Praise for *Sweetlust*

"Vivid yet nuanced, mysterious and sexy, each one of Asja Bakić's stories creates its own dangerous universe. This miraculous collection enraptured me again and again."
—CHANA PORTER, author of *The Seep*

"Haunting, funny, and delightfully surreal, *Sweetlust* pushes fiction into exciting and unexpected realms of imagination. A visceral dive into the perils and pleasures of the human condition."
—ADITI KHORANA, author of *The Library of Fates*

"In *Sweetlust*, Asja Bakić takes on gender, society, literature, climate change, and time travel with such extraordinary ease that one might be fooled into believing such mastery is easy. The narrative is quick and sharp while, almost deceptively, shedding strange and revelatory light on some of the most intimidating subjects of our age. Evocative of the work of Joyce Carol Oates and Leonora Carrington, Asja Bakić—aided by a brilliant translator—delivers a perfectly discordant punch to the gut of matters few dare touch. Truly fearless writing strikes real fear in the heart of a reader, and in this way, *Sweetlust* is a truly frightful book, and Asja Bakić a singular terror."
—LINA FERREIRA CABEZA-VANEGAS,
    author of *Don't Come Back*

"*Sweetlust* rollicks and seethes with a rakish energy, part hilarious, part bone-chilling. Translated brilliantly by Jennifer Zoble, these stories zip back and forth across the centuries. Never a dull moment!"
—ELLEN ELIAS-BURSAĆ, translator

sweetlust

Stories by Asja Bakić

Translated by Jennifer Zoble

THE FEMINIST PRESS
AT THE CITY UNIVERSITY OF NEW YORK
NEW YORK CITY

Published in 2023 by the Feminist Press
at the City University of New York
The Graduate Center
365 Fifth Avenue, Suite 5406
New York, NY 10016

feministpress.org

First Feminist Press edition 2023

This book was made possible thanks to a grant from the New York State Council
on the Arts with the support of the Governor and the New York State Legislature.

First printing February 2023

Cover design by Sukruti Anah Staneley
Photo by Siim Lukka on Unsplash
Text design by Drew Stevens

Library of Congress Cataloging-in-Publication Data

Names: Bakić, Asja, 1982- author. | Zoble, Jennifer, translator.
Title: Sweetlust / stories by Asja Bakić ; translated by Jennifer Zoble.
Other titles: Sladostrašće. English
Description: First Feminist Press edition. | New York City : The Feminist
    Press at the City University of New York, 2023.
Identifiers: LCCN 2022044580 (print) | LCCN 2022044581 (ebook) | ISBN
    9781952177729 (paperback) | ISBN 9781952177736 (ebook)
Subjects: LCGFT: Short stories.
Classification: LCC PG1420.12.A345 S5313 2023 (print) | LCC PG1420.12.A345
    (ebook) | DDC 891.8/3936—dc23/eng/20220915
LC record available at https://lccn.loc.gov/2022044580
LC ebook record available at https://lccn.loc.gov/2022044581

PRINTED IN THE UNITED STATES OF AMERICA

Contents

1998

SHE'D PLANNED TO stay home with her mother that summer until her father and sister returned from the European Junior Table Tennis Championships in Italy. Instead she spontaneously took a bus trip to Jablanica Lake with her friend Anida. Anida's mother was the secretary to the director of the postal service and sent them to a summer camp organized for the children of its employees. She was sixteen. She brought a two-piece bathing suit, teen angst, and the novel *I, Tituba, Black Witch of Salem* by Maryse Condé. She was looking forward to a perfect summer.

When she got off the bus, she realized she'd be sharing a tent with at least six other girls, which didn't particularly please her since she'd always found it difficult to make friends. She'd spent her life training at table tennis out of emotional obligations and habits, not because she enjoyed the company of others her age. Physical exertion made her feel good, but socializing exhausted her. She tended to expect the worst of people, primarily because players from the other team would always insult their opponents during matches to demoralize and weaken them. She dreamed of fair play, an atmosphere in which she'd be less anxious about losing. She was sensitive, but not in the same way as her peers. Anida, who was slightly younger, adored the film *Titanic*—she'd seen it at least twenty times. But she didn't share Anida's tastes, or even her sister's.

At the entrance to the camp, which was across from a lake, there were picnic tables where everyone ate. The kitchen was there, too, and next to that, a small infirmary. A hill rose above them. She knew right away that she'd spend most of her time up there; she was always looking for an isolated perch from which to study someone else's upbringing in order to forget about her own. Hordes of children packed into the same place was not an especially pleasant scenario for the organizers either. At times the racket seemed to reach all the way to the Amalfi Coast. But that wasn't her problem. Like any child, she needed a vacation from her own hormones, from the nightly growth of her breasts, which was driving her crazy. She loved other girls' tits. For herself she just wanted a straight line to death.

On the first day, right after breakfast, she climbed the hill and sat in the shade. Anida was going swimming with her friends and called out to her, of course, to join them. But she turned her down. She only went swimming at dusk, when there was no one left in the lake. She'd been watching them curiously from the hill. They may have shared the same tent, but they clearly didn't share the same thoughts: the other girls were obsessed with boys, and she couldn't bring herself to think about them. Still, she would occasionally wonder what she might be missing out on.

It was only on the third day that she dared to go in the lake with everyone else. A boy immediately grabbed her leg, wanting to start a conversation. It was a stupid, childish move, but she laughed. He was not repulsive to her. She swam away quickly nonetheless.

She experienced swimming differently from table tennis. For her it wasn't a sport. The nausea she woke up feeling on competition days disappeared in the lake water: she threw it to the muddy bottom with each crawl stroke. With each backstroke she unloaded the burden from her shoulders.

Shit! she thought. *I'm even competitive about intimate feelings.*

Everything in her world had become one big sports metaphor. Her muscular body carried her thoughts upstream, away from the tumult. She regarded the other swimmers with curiosity, like someone who had already beaten them at growing up, and at life. It was a sad gaze, but in the spirit

3

of victory, she had to move on. After swimming, she climbed the hill more slowly than usual. She'd brought her book but she didn't feel like cracking it open.

The reason why she hadn't gone to the European Junior Championships was trivial: the table tennis federation couldn't afford to pay for her travel as well as that of her colleagues. The two best teen-age girl athletes had stayed home. The kids in the younger division had gone; all the boys had gone. And it would've been fine (she was used to not having money) had she not, to her intense regret, reached an age when she could finally perceive the connection between money and men. She didn't want to think about it, but she had no choice.

That spring, the coach had invited her for fitness training camp. Everything that the boys' teams did, the girls would have to do, too, except there was no financial support. But they didn't tell her that before the trip. She ran for hours in sneakers with flimsy soles. She had blisters for days. Sometimes she squeezed her racket too hard, horrified by the thoughts that were bubbling to the surface, thoughts she couldn't make sense of. She needed to talk to the other girls. Who was crushing on whom was, of course, a common topic in the locker room, but the girls never complained about the poor conditions because there were always boys playing in the hallway outside, at the tables in the best locations, with the best lighting. The girls trained obediently

4

under flickering bulbs, on damaged floors. They showered and laughed together, but dreamed separately, each in her own room, steeped in lukewarm water and surging hormones. Perhaps it was then, as she watched her peers struggling to grow up, that her dissatisfaction asserted itself for the first time: Could a girl ever be important enough to be placed at the best table, beneath the best lights?

On the hill she could indulge the vice of thinking in peace. She sat up there until lunchtime, then went down among the other kids and chatted as much as she had to. Anida spoke loudly about the band The Kelly Family. She didn't know what to say in response. She preferred old Yugoslav pop songs. She could listen to Ivo Robić and Gabi Novak all day, but how to admit such a thing?

When lunch was over, the others retreated to the tent to rest. Near the lake was a large meadow that led to an overgrown forest. She set off on a hike. She felt free when she didn't have to watch what she was saying. She walked wherever she wanted. Just when she began searching for a spot where she could briefly lie down, she spotted in the distance the boy who'd touched her in the water. She ducked behind the nearest bush, hoping he hadn't seen her. Once she was convinced he wasn't following her, she got up and headed back to the camp. The kids had gone swimming. She sat by herself. Everything was all right.

In the evening she wanted to swim again. She

was most attracted to water when she couldn't see her reflection in it. She swam frantically, like she was racing. Suddenly, in the middle of the lake, someone pulled her by the leg. Twice, quite hard. She paused.

"Don't!" she said.

But when she turned, there was no one in the water.

THAT NIGHT, she couldn't sleep. She remembered her first fitness training in Hungary where, one night, in the cabin that housed all the girls, hundreds of cockroaches had fallen on their heads. Roaches had rained down from the ceiling at every angle. Wasn't this invasion of disgusting insects the perfect herald of a dangerous adolescence? She was thirteen then and looked like a boy. Even now, three years later, things hadn't changed that much. She hadn't gotten her period. She wasn't interested in boys. The picture she kept in her notebook wasn't a photo of the famous Hollywood actor Leonardo DiCaprio, but a portrait of the Partisan hero Rade Končar.

She listened to the other girls breathing in the tent. She didn't have a watch, but she could sense that dawn was approaching. The first rays of the sun put her to sleep. She didn't go to breakfast. She even slept through lunch.

At the lake, she and Anida spoke briefly about

table tennis. When summer was over, they'd have to start training again twice a day, sometimes for an exhausting six hours if the school allowed it. One hundred crunches, at least half an hour of running, and then stretching. She had to practice her spin and watch out for dangerous shots that opponents aimed at her torso. Her reflexes needed to be faster. Her wrists, more relaxed. She looked down at her legs: she was as agile as a cat, but twitchy. Her legs could not lessen the tension of her head. When she was depressed, not even a strong forehand could help. Her mood swings were visible to everyone. She didn't fit in. Maybe it wasn't such a bad thing that she played in poor lighting. Sports had sculpted her body, but the grimaces came from within, from a place she wanted to hide.

When she swam, time stood still. She stared down at the water: the surface of the lake thickened, grew more viscous. She swam with difficulty, as if through pancake batter. She felt herself becoming gooey, like a piece of dough changing shape. She wasn't scared; she'd always imagined growing up that way. The roar of the children around her continued unabated. She was the only one to notice what was happening. She knew such changes were necessary. In a couple of years she'd even love cabbage rolls: that's how deep the transformation would go.

As for Tituba, the Black witch of Salem, she delighted in her character: "Out of them all, you'll be the only one to survive." The first part of the novel ended with these words. She didn't dare read any further. The sun was beating down on her head. She set the book down on a towel and went back into the water. Surviving the first half of the nineties had been a real miracle. Surviving girlhood would be an even greater accomplishment. She admired herself for not bleeding. Nothing kept her from swimming. In high school, she never even missed gym class. Especially not when they were at the pool. The "women's problems" that plagued her had to do with the plot of Maryse Condé's novel, not with menstruation. The water didn't completely soothe her readerly unease, but she swam and swam. Had she continued at that pace, she could've crossed the Adriatic and gone to the competition in Italy. She was only sixteen, but she knew her efforts were insufficient. She could try her hardest, but it wouldn't stop her breasts from growing. She'd soon be crossing into puberty. Aging wasn't something you could postpone.

Out of them all, I'll be the only one not to survive, she thought.

She choked. She'd swallowed some lake water and it brought her back to reality. The young man was paddling his legs in the water. He observed her carefully. No one else seemed to pay him any attention. It was as if they didn't even see him. She knew he wasn't staying in the camp. No one in his family worked for the postal service. She dove down into the water. When she surfaced, he was gone. She

8

thought of the lake fairies who dragged men under. Maybe the young man would be their first victim this year?

DURING THE NIGHT she was awakened by a loud cry. The girl next to her had begun to bleed profusely. They helped her to her feet. Blood soaked her sleeping bag. Her sobs soon woke the rest of the girls. First they wadded some hand towels between her legs, then they switched to beach towels. Then they wrapped her in a sheet. When they saw that she wouldn't stop bleeding, they took her to the infirmary. The woman who worked there was awful. She asked the girl whom she'd slept with, whether she was a virgin or not. She yelled and insulted her. The girl was rapidly losing blood. The doctor on duty mentioned a miscarriage, then menorrhagia, which they'd never heard of. Ultimately the girl, wrapped in a sheet like a corpse, was thrown into a car—not an ambulance—and sent home, one hundred eighty kilometers away. The doctor didn't even bother to call her parents.

The whole tent reeked of blood. No one could go back to sleep. The girls were shuffled around to other areas of the campsite. She grabbed her sleeping bag, climbed the hill, and stretched out in the same spot where, earlier in the day, she'd sat thinking. Under the clear night sky, it suddenly occurred to her that the heavy bleeding hadn't been a gynecological problem. Something else was going on. She would have to find out what had happened to the girl.

Over the next five days, three more girls from her tent ended up in the infirmary. They were raced to Jablanica for a blood transfusion because all three had collapsed at the same time. Swaddled in blankets, they looked like rag dolls. Their parents needed to be notified of the incident, but the trip organizer wanted to cover it all up, lying to the mothers and fathers that it was simply anemia. When the girls returned to the camp, she noticed how much they had changed. Everyone pretended that nothing strange had happened, but the girls' faces looked different than they had before. She could clearly see the transformation. They still went swimming with Anida, but they walked strangely, as if they'd gone to a place that had turned them upside down.

Nothing bad happened to the boys in the meantime. For them, the summer was truly perfect. They played basketball and soccer. They swam, ate overstuffed bologna sandwiches, and thought about the girls—but also about the adult women who ran the camp.

"The things I'd do to her," she heard one say.

In her mind, those "things" could only mean going to the European Junior Championships instead of her, in her place.

"Gross!" she said.

The kid turned, the first hints of fuzz erupting from his upper lip.

"What are you whining about?" he shouted. "As if you wouldn't! Did you see those tits?!"

He thought he was addressing another boy. Then he looked at her more closely.

"I thought you were a guy," he said, confused.

She became a piece of dough again, and the ground on which she trod turned to water. She turned and swam away. Why did she lose to men every time? She wandered absently into the field and entered the woods. She walked, contemplating her own gender. How could you beat an opponent if you started the match with half the points already decided in his favor? You play until 21, and the scoreboard says 0–11. You haven't even taken your racket out of its case yet, and you're already losing.

She hiked for at least half an hour. Then she heard the sound of water. No one had mentioned this at the camp. Through a thick tangle of branches she spied a low waterfall cascading into a small pool. Beneath it was bathing a young man she instantly recognized. Actually, not bathing; only half of his body was in the waterfall. He looked as if he was stuck in the water, but he wasn't. She hardly blinked and he was gone. When she'd managed to get through the thicket, she went in the water. Unlike the lake, it was very cold. She nearly lost her breath. Not only her breath; the cold prolonged her entry into the waterfall, as if the moment when she'd stepped into the stream had been frozen. Then she felt a strong grip, like she had in the lake. This time someone seized her arm and pulled her under the waterfall. When she came out on the other side, she was greeted by an inverted image of the place she'd come from: the same stream, the same thicket. She walked through the same forest. For half an hour, just as she had on the way to the waterfall. Everything looked the same.

At the camp she saw the same people. It was lunchtime and everyone was sitting on picnic benches and eating. She looked around for Anida. As soon as she saw her, she went up to her.

"Scoot over," she said.

Anida shifted to make room for her. When she sat down, she carefully scrutinized her friend. How well did they know each other? She wasn't sure. Maybe she would be able to recognize the change in Anida, if only she would look her in the eye, but instead she kept her eyes on her plate, as if she knew. She chewed on the same slice of bread, it seemed, for hours.

"Are you looking forward to practice?" she asked Anida.

Her friend just stared ahead, replying, "Not really. It'll be hard to go back to school and train every day."

Okay, that sounded like something Anida would say. She wanted to ask her something more intimate, something that this Anida wouldn't know, but she needed to do it without making her suspicious.

"I haven't told anyone this, but at the tournament, A. gave me his track jacket."

"And?" asked her friend.

"I took it to my hotel room, locked the door, and put it on over my bare skin. I didn't tell you this, right?"

She waited for Anida's answer with great trepidation.

"No, this is the first I'm hearing it."

Her words were reassuring. Maybe she'd just imagined that this was the "wrong" Anida. They looked identical, and their voices sounded the same. But the doubt lingered, because her friend was gobbling up food from a plate that didn't seem to have emptied at all.

"Why aren't you eating anything?" Anida asked her with her mouth full.

"I'm not hungry. I'm going for a walk now, so I'll see you at the lake."

"Okay."

She didn't want to put anything from this world into her mouth. She'd read somewhere that when you eat something from the underworld, you get stuck there. She wanted to make sure she could still escape. But the longer she thought about her situation, the more her discomfort subsided. She climbed the hill, almost joyfully. The landscape was unchanged. In the tent, which did not smell of blood, she found her book. *Tituba* bore the familiar inscription from her sister; the handwriting was unmistakable. This world was real. She felt relieved. She was not nervous about talking to others. She slept peacefully that night. In the morning she had fun swimming.

Just a little more, she told herself. *An hour or two and then I'll go back*. But she couldn't bring herself to leave.

Things were better for her here. She felt good in her own skin. She didn't think about Italy or table tennis. It was as if she'd offloaded her trauma. The next day, without any apprehension, she started talking about music while everyone was playing in the lake.

"Do any of you listen to old Yugoslav music from the sixties?" she asked. She was proud of herself.

"Like Gabi Novak?"

"Yes!" she said. "Doesn't she have an amazing voice?"

"She does," someone said.

It was Anida's turn to reply. She was expecting the same lecture she'd heard from her friend a hundred times: There was no band like The Kelly Family. Everyone else was garbage.

"I like Tic Tac Toe the most," said Anida.

Saying this, her friend finally looked her right in the eye. A smile flickered across her lips. There was something awful about the way her mouth twisted, as if half her face were paralyzed.

Moving slowly away from Anida, she gave a

laugh. Her heart was pounding in panic, but she knew that she mustn't show any fear. This place, whatever it was, had sucked her in, and there was no need to further provoke it.

"I'm getting hungry," Anida said. "Do you want a sandwich?"

She wanted to slowly disappear from Anida's sight and run back to the waterfall. She'd stayed here too long.

"I was thinking of eating too," she said, maintaining her smile. "Can I get you something from the kitchen?"

She wouldn't give up. She refused to let Anida come along. How would she ditch someone who was following her?

"Okay," Anida said.

She took two sandwiches and headed back to the lake. She gave one to Anida, and then threw the other in the bushes.

"I'm going up the hill to finish my book."

She went to the tent, grabbed *Tituba*, and hurried out. The book was her only proof.

"Where are you?" she heard Anida's voice in the distance.

She was a long way from camp now and knew she shouldn't stop. Even one step backward would be an act of insanity.

"Frieeeeeeeeeeeeeeeeend!"

The drawn-out crackling of Anida's voice sounded like someone setting up a radio antenna. She quickened her pace.

"Let's plaaaaaaaaaaaay!"

She heard the sound of a rumbling stomach. The footsteps behind her resounded more and more clearly. She ran. She shoved the book down her pants to free up her hands. She parted the branches and ran as if she weren't a table tennis player but a track athlete. Her knees buckled in fear. She didn't want the fake Anida to catch up with her and send a doppelgänger in her place. When she finally reached the waterfall, she turned and saw that, instead of her friend, the young man she'd seen at the lake was staring at her.

"Where are you rushing off to?" he asked.

He stood still. He didn't go into the water after her. He figured he didn't have to.

"You look like a guy," he said.

"I know."

"I don't mind."

"I don't mind either," she said.

"You're lying."

Before the trip through the waterfall, that would've been true, but she wasn't lying now. She didn't care what she looked like. She just wanted to survive. That was the most important thing to her. She said to him, "The fact that you didn't know her favorite band gave you away."

He laughed. And his stomach growled again. His voracious mouth widened into an even bigger smile.

"Do you want to eat me?" she asked.

"Just below the waist." He fixed her with his gaze. "You have nice muscular legs. Nice thighs."

It didn't sound like he was describing a drumstick. Maybe his appetite was different?

"Why are you so hungry?"

The answer hung in the air. She watched his every move. It helped that she'd had practice reading other people in table tennis. She'd often seen people using their hands to hide the setup of their serves in order to confuse her. When she got back home, when she survived this, she'd train for seven hours, go running, exercise like crazy. She wanted to read her future opponents like an open book.

The young man didn't budge. He just stood still and watched her. So she stood motionless too. She was careful not to turn her back to him.

"I wonder what you did to the other girls."

"I made them happy, that's all," he said.

"I wouldn't call bleeding 'happy.'"

"Blood is the consequence of great fun."

"Yours, perhaps," she said.

"Don't be cruel. If they weren't having fun, they wouldn't have kept coming back. If anyone was hungry, it was them."

He shrugged as if indifferent, but his face twitched. This discussion was wearing him out.

"You're stubborn. Don't you feel relieved that you're here?" he asked.

"I do, and that worries me the most. Problems don't just disappear like that."

"You sound like a precocious child," he said. "You don't know what you're talking about."

"Unfortunately I do."

He grinned, but in agony. If he made even the slightest movement, his prey would escape, and then what would he do? Play with himself? Where was the pleasure in that?

"We can stand together here under the waterfall—we don't have to touch. I just want to get close to you."

A shiver passed through her. She was sure he would grab her at any moment and drag her into the woods.

"You're different, better than the other girls," he said.

She laughed. She knew she wasn't better. That realization would save her.

"They were the appetizer?"

"Yes!"

Now her stomach began to growl. She had to get out of there. She was overcome with lust. Her stomach grew louder. Her knees buckled, but not from fear.

"You're not really my taste," she said with great difficulty, stepping back. "After practice, I could eat a whole fridge. You're just scraps."

"Clever!" he yelled. "This isn't over."

He ran into the water after her, but her athletic reflexes saved her. She ducked under the waterfall. He grabbed her by the arm, but she slipped through his grasp. She fell hard in the shallow water, breaking her nose. Survival wasn't elegant. The book got wet. Her sister's inscription bled across the paper like a common stain.

When she arrived back at the camp, the sun had already set. The kids were sitting around a fire. Anida was telling jokes. She looked at them all briefly and then, when her breathing had finally calmed down, she took a triumphant step toward the infirmary. She was happy there was no blood running down her legs.

Gretel

A glitch is the loss of control.
  —OLGA GORIUNOVA, "GLITCH"

US

There were no more men. All that remained of them was Sweetlust. When the amusement park opened in Karlovac over fifteen years ago, the whole country raced to it. Sweetlust became the main place for socializing and spending money, and all the women, including my best friends, couldn't wait to take part. The park paid no taxes to the state because it was registered as a rehabilitation center for women with scoliosis. Its director, curator Karla L, carefully programmed a series of erotic activities for visitors to enjoy day and night. All of the activities were, of course, conventionally heterosexual. The media nonetheless deemed them "revolutionary." In front of the entrance hall were stands selling sausages called "girl dreams," sex toys (the most popular of which was a small chip that visitors placed under the skin of their groin for enhanced pleasure in the park's virtual worlds), and popcorn and cotton candy in everyone's favorite shade of pink.

"Isn't it sad to be surrounded by other women but still thinking only about men?" I asked one of my friends.

"We're mourning them," she said.

"But it's been years! Sweetlust keeps us stuck in the past. Isn't it time to move on?"

"It's still too soon."

My friends planned a trip to the amusement park for International Women's Day. I'd stubbornly refused to go with them in years past. But this time, instead of the usual lecture about how March 8 had nothing to do with "girl dreams," nail polish, or candy apples, my friends heard only my brusque "yes" and were left stunned by the unexpected capitulation.

"You'll really go?" they asked.

"Yes," I repeated. "It's time."

There wasn't much on the internet about the park in Karlovac and the fun that awaited women there. If someone wrote something about their experience, it was just their general impressions: what the weather was like, how the people were. No one ever elaborated because visitors had to sign a nondisclosure agreement upon entering. The curator hoped to emulate the Eleusinian Mysteries: only those women who came in person would know exactly what happened and what the rites of the Karlovački initiation were like.

My friends had signed the NDA, but they nevertheless spilled every detail. They were somehow still attached to me, though exactly why was no longer clear: they'd spent every free moment at the park since its opening, and we'd begun to drift apart. While they went for "rehabilitation," I devised my revenge: a computer virus I wrote in secret. I wanted to attack Karlovac with a big zero to nullify the damage caused by its message, but I knew this wasn't possible. I needed to cast the ones and zeros slowly—bit by bit, as if flicking pubic hairs one at a time into sterile enemy territory. I programmed day and night in hopes of deprogramming my friends and all those poor, naive women who traveled to the park seeking a dose of mystery and left their hard-earned money there.

The thrills the park offered were, in my opinion, very banal. According to my friends, every room had a story that each woman could inhabit with abandon. The park cooperated closely with Google and social media, and visitors were thoroughly profiled using data from their online searches, purchases, and TV and film viewing habits. But the personalization was a lie. The women were alienated from themselves and from the algorithm.

At the same time, the false pleasure sold to visitors destroyed Karlovac, transforming it into a witch's house covered in chocolate and cake.

Every woman who made a pilgrimage there was a Hansel to be fattened up, shoved into an oven, and devoured. I decided to call the virus I'd written "Gretel."

"Wear something nice," my friends told me. "You need to look hot."

"I will," I said, even though I didn't see why I should get dressed up for artificial intelligence.

Not many people were aware that *L* wasn't the first letter of Karla's last name, but rather the Roman numeral fifty. Before her, the men had tested out forty-nine other versions of Karla, but I suspected they'd then written a special program that wouldn't need to be translated into a low-level assembly language. Rumors spread that Karla L had in fact programmed herself using a machine language that people couldn't understand at all. At first I'd been skeptical, but such gossip wasn't always unfounded.

The men had originally wanted to build the park in Duga Resa, but they'd ultimately given up the idea because they needed more space for the servers. The Mrežnica River was insufficient for cooling them, so Karlovac—"the City on Four Rivers"—was the perfect location. Beneath the city unfurled a network of tunnels and cellars that housed the legion of servers. Karla L monitored everything, including the master server. My plan was to act like an arrogant and overexcited visitor and bulldoze my way into a more exclusive package for me and my friends. Then I'd separate from the group to perform my mission: uploading Gretel to some of the terminals and letting her pump through the virtual reality that visitors paid outlandish prices for. Paradoxically, the VR packages that Karla L sold included cultural material that belonged to all of us. Fairy tales, Jane Austen novels, adaptations of books and comics that previous generations had effortlessly enjoyed for free had suddenly become exclusive content costing an arm and a leg because it was "personalized."

Karla L ranked the offerings on her menu by popularity: the most famous programs instantly became the most expensive. Everyone knew in principle what "Beauty and the Beast" was about, so Karla L made it the most sought-after experience. Every woman, the amusement park claimed, wanted a beast she could save and tame for her own sexual pleasure.

"That sounds terrible," I told my friend.

"It's really fun!" she said. "The Beast's appearance is tailored to your desires. They know exactly what will cause the most pleasure and what kind of Beast will make you emotionally invested."

"And intellectually?" I asked.

"Don't be silly," she said. "No one goes to Karlovac to talk."

"But how can you get turned on without conversation?"

"With a look, with flirty hints. Touch. Women aren't fools," she said.

At that moment I wasn't so sure.

"Sex can't rehabilitate anyone, not even those with a crooked spine," I spat.

"The scoliosis thing is just a cover," she said.

I was glad the park hadn't completely brainwashed her.

"Tax exemptions," she added. "You know how these things work."

Of course I knew. The same multinational corporation controlled all amusement parks like Sweetlust. The content offered varied from country to country: the stories and situations that aroused—that is, "rehabilitated"—Serbian women were allegedly different from those favored by, for instance, Croatian women, Uruguayan women, or American women. The wealthier the country, the better the product. Pleasure was mapped out in advance: everything was categorized, documented, and priced in different currencies.

"You'll see," my friend said. "Nothing compares with the desire you're about to experience. It's impossible to describe."

Early in the morning on March 8, we arrived in Karlovac. Snow was falling, but everyone was dressed lightly. Wrapped in their coats, my friends walked through the snow in open-toed heels, in the kind of makeup you'd wear to an evening gala, not a dark space where visitors stuck VR goggles on their heads and crawled around fondling imaginary male genitalia with palms drenched in spit and sweat. The park recorded the highest numbers of visitors on weekends and holidays, which explained the crowd of women patiently waiting at the entrance. In front of the main gate a video played in which Karla L invited her guests to relax and enjoy the greatest entertainment in the world. Her artificial face filled me with discomfort. It reminded me too much of a dealer, a hustler, someone who'd coax the last dinar from my pocket just to humiliate me.

As I sidled up to the admission kiosk, the video glitched. The screen froze with Karla L looking right at me. It lasted so briefly as to be barely detectable, but I didn't believe in coincidences like that. Not anymore. I wasn't paranoid, rather, prepared for the worst, and my worst-case scenario was apocalyptic. I turned my gaze to the cashier as if I hadn't noticed anything.

"Welcome!" repeated the voice of Karla L. "Welcome!"

Visitors didn't know that Karla L was artificial intelligence. I wasn't sure if it had ever been discussed in public. The media held their silence. Her character was necessary to motivate women to be ambitious, successful, and carefree. She promised wonders, and had to be made of flesh and blood so that women would recognize themselves in her. The mission of Karla L to make all women happy needed to be natural in order to be effective. Compared to her story, Gretel sounded deviant, like something that had crawled up from the depths of hell. For every "sweetlustful" corporate image of the self-sacrificing woman who could enjoy life only after healing a wounded, misunderstood man-beast, I could respond only with the dirty, unappealing truth that love never healed anyone. Women had become obsessed with the idea of a romantic love that would free them from all negative emotions. They'd forgotten that emotions like fear were essential to survival. The body feared with reason.

"Relax," my friends said.

I was afraid for myself, but for them too. Their denial saddened me.

Karla L wasn't your typical villain. Other women had tried to hack her (I wasn't the first to despise her), but we'd quickly perceived that efforts to destroy her through outside programming were in vain: we were throwing eggs at a stone fortress. After months of contemplating how to deal with her, I realized that instead of striking Karla L herself, I needed to subvert what she relied on: her own lie. Once I became conscious of the fact that I was dealing with a story, everything became easier. I was less fearful. As with any ugly story, I could remake Sweetlust, rewrite it more beautifully. In my version, women would no longer cry for men when they came. Sweetlust advertised those tears as a catharsis, a sign of healing, but my Gretel would reveal what they really were: a symptom of widespread chronic depression.

As soon as I paid the entry fee, a guide separated me and my friends from the mass of other women.

We'd bought the full package, which included VIP treatment: we could go wherever we wanted. Of course, such freedom of movement was a lie because there was no way we could get to the server. I had the right to move only in virtual reality, not outside of it. All you could see was the set—never the scaffolding.

"Look," one of my friends said. "Girl dreams! Buy one, get one free."

"Considering how much money we paid to get in, I wouldn't say anything at that stand is 'free.'"

"Soon you'll be coming so hard you won't think about money for ten years."

Her words sounded like a threat.

"I don't like crying in public," I said.

"You need to shed a tear or two."

Before I could continue arguing, we arrived at the first of the thirteen rooms we were supposed to visit that weekend. I wasn't enthusiastic—I didn't miss men in the slightest—but my friends were jumping for joy.

"We begin gently," I heard the voice of Karla L coming from a small screen next to the door.

In the first room, a historical romance awaited us. I guessed that Karla L had adapted a best seller by Julie Garwood or Judith McNaught, but I wasn't sure. My virus was supposed to turn every visitor to this story into a servant who spent hours handwashing a nobleman's codpiece. I'd enjoyed coming up with that twist, but before I had the chance to chuckle at my own cleverness, my friends surrounded me: two of them took me by the hand, and the third produced a small chip from somewhere and placed it behind my ear. I looked at them, astonished.

"What did you do?" I asked nervously.

My friends were also programmers. Two worked for Google, and the other for the Ministry of the Interior. All three, like me, had been hackers in their student days. I'd thought they were ashamed of their past, but obviously I'd been mistaken.

"Doesn't that chip go near my crotch?" I asked.

"Not this one," one of them whispered.

She winked at me, putting her finger to her lips. I needed to be quiet. It was pretty dark in the room, but I could still make out that they were adjusting their watches. They fastened one of them on my wrist.

"After this, we'll go right to the thirteenth room, for 'Beauty and the Beast,'" they said.

I was about to take Gretel from my pants pocket, but my friends shook their heads. They were planning something. I was thrilled. I touched the chip behind my ear. My friend smiled.

"Relax," she said loudly. "When the sex is amazing, nothing else matters, right?"

"You're right," I said, even louder.

I came, it's true, but I wasn't happy about it. It was difficult to concentrate on the task at hand when the clitoris was in charge: my soul had plunged into it. The virtual reality was attending to my pulsating anus. Very actively. It didn't distinguish one hole or nerve ending from another. Karla L was thorough, I had to give her that much.

When we were led to the second room, my friends stopped the guide and told her we should go directly to the last room.

"It's our friend's first time here and we want her to experience only the best. Today's her birthday."

Their lie was persuasive and the guide believed them.

"Let me just notify Karla L," she said.

"Of course!"

My friends were brilliant. They'd come to Sweetlust often and I finally understood why. They'd wept so many times under the watchful eye of Karla L that they aroused no suspicion. They'd persisted in their performance for years.

"You're our Trojan horse," they murmured while we waited for the guide to return with an answer. "Be patient."

I trusted them, but the feeling of sadness was more palpable.

"All right," said the smiling guide when she came back. "Karla L approved the change. Come with me."

We followed her to a velvet door. The door alone was enough to make a woman come: it was soft, like a pincushion. Karla's greeting for us waited on a monitor to the left.

"Welcome!" she said.

This one hadn't been recorded in advance.

"Your friend's celebrating her birthday?"

"Yes," they said.

"It appears there's been a mistake. My records don't show her birthday as International Women's Day."

"That's our inside joke," said one of my friends. "We celebrate the birthdays we choose for ourselves. I, for example, was born in February, but I celebrate my birthday in July."

Our joke didn't have a digital trail, which confused Karla L. Everything had a trail. Everything.

"All right," she said, sounding unconvinced.

She wished me a happy birthday and our eyes met again, but this time Karla L maintained complete control over her code.

"Enjoy!"

We entered one by one. As soon as the door had closed, my friends swapped the chip behind my ear for another.

"We don't have a lot of time," they said. "Keep her occupied. Good luck!"

HER

"Wait!" I yelled to them, but they could no longer hear me.

What did "keep her occupied" mean? My throat clenched from rising tears. I'd never cried because of a man, but my friends were my weak spot. Nothing confirmed for me that I was a woman more powerfully than my complicated, often difficult relationships with other women. This could perhaps explain my impulse to instantly, without any deliberation, accept my role in a plan I knew nothing about. I'd worked doggedly on Gretel, but now that I needed to choose between my own vision and friendship, it was as if Gretel had ceased to exist. Just two words from my friends had been enough to make me give up on myself.

I waited for the computer to generate the setting and my avatar, hoping that my haste wasn't going to cost me my head. Not only was I in the dark about my friends' intentions, I also had no idea what Karla L would try to do with me.

I assumed that my friends hadn't clued me into their plan because I wasn't a good liar. My face was an open book; Karla L would read me easily. I was sometimes, truth be told, too direct for the political games that were a daily indulgence for employees of the ministry and Google, but didn't I deserve even the slightest hint? I stood in the virtual reality anteroom, completely lost. It seemed Sweetlust brought out the worst in all of us. I waited to see from which direction danger would strike me first. Men were no longer with us, but their shadow hung over everything. That enormous shadow tended to blur the contours of women's faces. Sometimes it seemed that the women who'd come to power had begun to resemble men. I didn't want to think about my friends this way.

The world without men wasn't the utopia we'd

longed for. After the entire male population died of syphilis, women at first had felt a weight lifted from their hearts, but with Sweetlust they'd soon transferred that weight to their backs. The amusement park was the crown jewel in the final stage of men's lunacy, but women embraced it as the loveliest memory of the extinct gender. They walked bent beneath the banal epitaph.

There was no cure for syphilis because the bacteria *Treponema pallidum* mutated beyond recognition. Not one woman succumbed to the deadly infection, but its madness spread to us. A destructive idea can be more dangerous than bacteria. Karla L knew this all too well. On the outside, women were infected with her optimism, but inside they wrestled with a guilty conscience for identifying with *T. pallidum*: they were the spirochetes that had obliterated men with sex. The more often they went to Sweetlust, the more convinced they became of their guilt. Hadn't men written for centuries about long feminine hair, prophetically describing women as "an irresistible sickness"? Had their misogyny not been justified? Women cried and came, came and cried, for nearly twenty years. I wanted to help them finish the business of wailing once and for all. But it looked like my friends had beaten me to the punch.

When the virtual reality was finally loaded, I looked around. I was in a garden full of roses. Since I'd read the classic fairy tale, I wasn't surprised. You were supposed to pluck a rose to summon the

Beast. It wasn't entirely clear in this case, frankly, whether I was the Beauty or the Beast. Before I dared to touch a rosebush and discover the truth, I went walking. Right away I noticed that the castle had been replaced with a modern one-story glass house. There was a pool in front of it. The sun was shining. I wore a bathing suit and was wrapped in a beach towel. Nothing in this world was to my taste.

I grabbed a rose and cut myself on a thorn. From the bush emerged Karla L. I was expecting her, but I nonetheless recoiled at the sight of her: She looked like a woman dipped in a sugar glaze. She reminded me of a candied apple.

"Which of us is the Beast?" I asked her.

Karla L just smiled secretively and shrugged.

"Can you at least explain why neither of us is a man?"

"Maybe the chip your friends gave you has something to do with it."

"What chip?" I asked. "I don't know what you're talking about."

She approached me and took the chip from behind my ear.

"This one."

She shoved it under my nose.

"They gave me that to intensify my orgasms. I've never been here before, so I don't know where it normally goes."

Karla L smiled again. She slid the chip into her bra.

"Don't defend them," she said. "I'm intimately

acquainted with all women. Deceit is encoded in your DNA."

Her response immediately clarified which of us was the Beast.

"I was born a man," I said. "Your theory doesn't hold water."

"Why would anyone want to become a woman? That's incredibly stupid."

"But you're a woman," I replied.

"This is just an avatar," she said with a dismissive wave.

"What do you look like when you have no audience?" I asked.

I expected Karla L to take on a different, masculine form then, but she didn't relinquish her facade.

"That's irrelevant," she said.

Now I shrugged. I feigned indifference. But I was afraid.

"It's a shame your friends' plan didn't work," she said.

"I don't know what the plan was, but I doubt it had anything to do with you."

"Nonsense," said Karla L. "Everything at Sweetlust has to do with me."

I had no idea what my friends had planned, but I didn't want the AI to know that. I didn't want to reveal my greatest weakness.

"They wanted to use you," she said.

"Possibly."

Gretel was in my pocket, but since I was nearly

naked in this world, I couldn't find the pocket. I regretted that this hadn't occurred to me sooner.

"What made you visit the park now?" Karla L asked.

Her curiosity surprised me.

"So you don't know everything after all."

"I know," she said angrily, "but I want to hear it from your lips."

"It was time."

"Time for what?" she asked.

"To kill you," I replied.

Karla L laughed. She hadn't expected an honest answer.

"You see, not all women lie," I said.

"You're not a woman," Karla L said.

"If I weren't a woman, I'd be dead."

That silenced her for a moment.

"Either way, if you were born a man, you can't be a real woman."

I was seized by choking, nervous laughter.

"Why are you laughing like that? Stop!" said Karla L.

My fear slowly transformed into anger. I remembered the pubic hair. Bit by bit, I kept telling myself. Bit by bit. I needed to outwit her—that was all. I had to keep her talking.

"If I'm not a real woman and I'm not a dead man, what am I, then?" I asked her.

"An enigma."

"Weren't women always enigmas to men?"

"I'm not a man," said the AI.

"But your chauvinism is definitely male."

I was trying to lead her onto thin ice.

"Otherwise, why would I be wearing a bathing suit?" I continued. "Why would I look like this?"

"That's what you yourself wanted," Karla L replied.

"Nothing here is to my liking," I said. "This is someone else's cheap fantasy."

To her I was the Beast. I saw that she couldn't fully understand my words. She froze, barely capable of continuing the conversation.

"What do you want?" she asked.

"What every woman wants."

"You miss men? You want them back?"

"No," I said.

"What do you want, then? What do women want?" asked Karla L.

"We want to bury men once and for all," I heard my friends say.

Karla L turned around in panic. Neither she nor I could see them.

"Impossible!" she shouted.

We were both in the dark, but there was no time to give in to disappointment. I got up in her face. Karla L took a step back, then two more. She was getting close to the rosebushes and their perilous thorns.

"Men died long ago—there's no need for women to keep crying over them day after day. We've mourned long enough."

"But women adore Sweetlust!" said Karla L. "Women love me!"

"Women hate Sweetlust!" said my friends.

When she wasn't looking, I grabbed Karla L by the neck.

WHAT MY FRIENDS did then wasn't entirely clear. I assumed that the chip Karla L had hidden in her cleavage really did have something to do with the whole intervention. I asked my friends afterward, when it was all over, to explain everything in detail.

"How did I manage to strangle Karla L?" I asked.

"That's classified," said my friend who worked at the ministry.

I had indeed served them like a virus. I'd written Gretel, but in the end I myself had played her role.

"Biology defeated technology. How is that even possible?" I asked.

"Information is information. There's no substantive difference between biology and technology," said my friend from Google.

Her tone was patronizing. I felt a bit stupid.

Now there were no more men, and no more Sweetlust. We could start anew, just like my friends said. No longer covered by a fake roof of candy. All around us were bare walls and exhausted women leaning against them. Some of the visitors lay on the floor and we had to step over them on our way to the exit. Our teeth chattered from the cold.

"They got their first dose of antibiotics," said one of my friends. "Everything will be okay."

"We won," said another.

I didn't share their optimism. I looked down at the weeping women we were stepping over.

"Sadness can't be turned off like a computer," I said as we arrived at the parking lot.

My friends pretended they hadn't heard me. We drove home in complete silence.

Blindness

"WHAT GOD CONCEALS, sex reveals," my sister said.

I thought she was driving me to Međugorje, but she had a different plan.

"There's a nasty storm coming—we left at just the right time," she continued.

The anticipation in her voice was palpable.

"Isn't it better to drive in nice weather?" I asked.

"I prefer rain," she said, stepping on the gas.

Her window was down and the wind was ruffling our hair. It wasn't blowing hard, but I could tell it was going to get worse. We both listened carefully to the forecast. The rain didn't matter—what excited my sister was the thunderstorm slowly moving inland. I closed my eyes as she described the sky. My mind halted at the color blue; I'd begun to forget it. It took me a moment to understand what my sister was talking about. Colors were growing more and more abstract. They were harder for me to imagine than God.

NEARLY TWO YEARS before, I had lost my sight. Quite suddenly. My sister had taken me to various doctors, with no results. My eyes were totally normal. Neither the ophthalmologists nor the neurologists could find the cause of my blindness. I'd suffered no physical injury: no fateful blow to the head, no tumble down a manhole. No one in my family had ever gone blind. Darkness had simply descended from nowhere and, panic-stricken, I struggled to escape. After consulting the doctors I went on various pilgrimages, first to Marija Bistrica because it was closest, and then wherever else I could think to go. I visited all the monasteries in Serbia, Montenegro, and Croatia, all the hodže and imams in Bosnia, and even one rabbi in Zagreb. In Zavidovići, they performed molybdomancy on me, read the beans, blew in my ears. A woman from Subotica told me to put two nails under my pillow every night to drive away the Devil, but my sister wouldn't hear of it. She didn't believe in God and she despised priests, but she took me to see them anyway. I didn't lose hope. I carried amber prayer beads in one pocket, a rosary in the other. My sister sewed talismans onto my clothes.

"It's all nonsense," she said. "If Yugoslavia hadn't fallen apart, we would have decent doctors. Communists would be able to help you see again."

Whenever my sister would open her mouth to spit on God, I would recite a prayer or two to silence her.

"Hail Mary, full of grace . . ."

My sister was named Marija, and I felt like I was also praying to her.

It was difficult, getting used to being blind. For the first three months, I cried incessantly and prayed to God to either restore my sight or take my life. My sister got me a cane and a guide dog. They didn't help though, because fear and shame kept me from leaving the house. Of all the senses, I'd always valued sight the most. So when I lost it, it was as if I'd lost my legs. I sat by the window all day, in complete darkness regardless of the time. I sobbed loudly on purpose, so all the neighbors could hear.

"Enough!" snapped my sister. "It's time to move on."

To punish her, I vowed to seek answers in seminaries and monasteries. Without hesitating, she filled up the tank and we set off for Marija Bistrica. That pilgrimage didn't help either, but once I got going, it was hard to stop me. I wanted to travel, and my sister spent weekends in her car anyway. She was constantly escaping from home, escaping from me. Now I began to escape with her.

THE DAY BEFORE I went blind, I'd masturbated for the very first time in my life. I was in the bed my grandmother used to sleep in. Above me hung a fragile ceramic crucifix. I came abruptly and Jesus fell to the floor, shattering. I didn't say a word to my sister. The next night I lost my vision.

Marija sometimes went to Bosnia, so she remembered that there was a Franciscan monastery in Jajce. After Bistrica we went there, but instead of seeking help, we visited the bones of the last Bosnian king, Stjepan Tomašević. I couldn't see him, but my sister described him succinctly.

"He's very small," she said.

I felt nothing when I touched his glass coffin. My sight was not restored. It was at that moment that I began to doubt God. I felt ashamed, so the whole ride home I prayed. I gripped my rosary and thought of the Virgin. I understood Marija. Not my sister Marija, rather the Virgin Mary. I never managed to understand my sister. We were very different. She was a grumpy librarian, and I avoided literature because I feared it had made her that way, that books had ruined her life. While Marija went to the library, I sought out nature, far away from the literary heroes she served more devoutly than I did Jesus.

Once, when she wasn't home, I took a peek at her personal library. She had books by the Marquis de Sade, whom I'd heard terrible things about at school. He was surely burning in hell. I opened one of his books right to the sentence: *Virtue, vice, all are confounded in the grave.*

My sister had underlined it. She'd also marked: *Oh! let her fuck with impunity!*

As I lay in bed, I thought about what I'd read. Before going to sleep I prayed, and then my hand lowered itself between my legs and waited for something. Then Jesus fell from the wall, and I lost my sight.

THE CAR WAS speeding along the slick road, but my sister was an excellent driver and I wasn't afraid. I had complete confidence in her. I wanted to drive one hundred sixty kilometers an hour, or even faster. Had I been behind the wheel, we would've traveled at the speed of light because I wanted to get to our destination as soon as possible. I felt deep down that we weren't really going to Međugorje. God did not want me to go to Herzegovina and lose my faith forever.

When I could still see, I'd often gone on field trips to the Neretva Valley with the department of experimental biology. I was a freshman in the faculty of sciences and I wanted to study botany for the rest of my life, pressing delicate flowers into notebooks and aromatic herbs into my bra, as my grandmother had. When she'd hugged me to her chest, I could smell the mint leaves or rose petals she'd stuffed where other women would put nylon

45

stockings. My grandmother was also a Marija, so whenever I uttered the name of the Mother of God, I spoke of her too. They both were in my heart. I kept my sister further south, where sisters should never be. Maybe that's why Jesus fell from the wall and broke into pieces.

We didn't actually drive for that long. I hadn't even gotten the urge to use the bathroom yet, and we were already turning off the highway.

"Where are we?" I asked my sister.

"In Gorska Hrvatska."

I knew that mountainous terrain well.

"What part?"

"In the part where you'll see again," my sister said.

My anticipation was growing. My hands began to shake.

"So, it's definitely not Lika," I said.

Marija didn't reply; she just kept driving. I couldn't ascertain the exact time, but we'd set out in the morning. I fell deep into thought, imagining the miracle that would bring back my sight. My sister put on Bebi Dol, a singer we both loved. She wanted me to relax, but I was already relaxed enough. When we stopped, I heard Marija open her backpack and pull out a book. Without warning, she began to read aloud.

"'At the top of the steps, the path arrives at a ridge. From one side rises another path that climbers take, but our path proceeds along the ridge first,

46

past the memorial stones for the dead climbers, and then ascends to the summit. Even though the last part of the ascent is a challenge, and sometimes requires the use of hands to climb it, there aren't any serious difficulties. It's dangerous only during rainfall, when the rocks are slippery. One should not get too close to the edge. The rounded peak is ten meters in diameter. It affords sweeping views of Gorski kotar in one direction, and in another, one can see all the way to Medvednica, above Zagreb. Here one should take particular care not to cause falling rocks, which can be deadly for climbers below.'"

At that point she stopped, inhaled, and closed the book. I was seized by panic.

"You want me to climb to the top of a mountain?" I asked, dumbfounded.

"Yes," my sister said.

"But I can't see anything!"

"I know."

When we got out of the car, it was drizzling. The wind was picking up speed. I could easily imagine the stormy sky above us.

"Where are we?" I asked.

"In the foothills," Marija said.

"Be specific!"

My sister said this was the only pilgrimage I needed.

"I've spent a lot of time studying the trail. I'll tie you to me, and we'll climb it together."

"But the book says it's dangerous!"

"Sight is a dangerous sense," said my sister.

I stopped protesting. Marija removed her climbing equipment from the trunk. We put on boots and windbreakers. My sister put a helmet on my head, and then one on her own.

"You know, if we fall from the top, this won't be of much use," I said.

"You need to reach the top first."

She was right. My sister was always right.

"Who are these climbers who died, anyway? When did they die?" I asked.

"The first one died in 1927. And then there were three more."

"And now the two of us, except that no one will build us a monument," I said, resigned.

I wasn't angry.

"Why don't you pray to God to help us," Marija said.

She laughed. The rain began to fall harder.

"Let's go—we need to get there before dark, and the trail is brutal."

I noticed that she didn't give me a backpack to carry. Maybe she didn't expect us to survive. That thought calmed me even more than Bebi Dol. My sister hooked the rope to my climbing harness.

"I don't need a guide dog when I have you," I said.

Marija was silent.

"Have I been here before? For school?" I asked.

"Yes, you have."

This narrowed the possibilities a bit.

"Do I have a souvenir from here?"

I was referring to plants. She understood.

"Of course. You never come home empty-handed. Even when you should."

Suddenly before my eyes, against the black screen of my blindness, appeared, like a light-house, my favorite species, *Primula kitaibeliana*. Its thick, sticky hairs, and its pink flowers poking out from craggy limestone cliffs, had always delighted me. The plant needed just a little land; it thrived in meager conditions, cold and barren soil, damp. Kitaibel's Primrose was plant perfection. As I watched it, it clung to my palate; I could almost feel it blooming in my pharynx. Not even the body of Christ had such intoxicating power. As soon as that thought occurred to me, I crossed myself in panic. I hadn't even taken three steps and already I was blaspheming.

"You brought me to Klek," I said quietly. "To the witches' mountain."

"And where else?" my sister replied.

We climbed slowly. There was no one else on the trail. The storm had cleared our path.

"Be careful not to step on any plants," Marija said.

Since I couldn't see where I was going, I spent most of the hike on my hands and knees, feeling my way along. My sister didn't help me much. We climbed in silence. Maybe she was trying to punish me. The Klek massif was the perfect revenge for all those pilgrimages, all those monasteries she'd reluctantly accompanied me to. I was hoping that at any moment she would stop climbing and admit that she just wanted to scare me, but the journey continued, as did her silence. I feared for my life, but at the same time I was very excited. The hair on my body grew sticky; it was thrilling to climb on my knees to the perilous summit. I'd always loved Klek. Not only because of the primroses, but also the beautiful view. Grandma Marija was born in Ogulin and had always enjoyed telling us about scaling the mountain slopes. She'd never mentioned any dead climbers, but she must've known about them. Nor had she ever mentioned the witches' dance. She didn't want to scare us.

My sister Marija, on the other hand, lived for fear. She loved literature because she was morbid. While I'd run through the fields and pick flowers, she'd sit in the shade and read Gothic and romance novels. She had a wild, romantic imagination and aimed to consume each book as if it were one of Grandma's cakes. Sometimes she would get so engrossed in a story that I could put a wreath of flowers on her head without her even noticing. In the first grade, she'd been scolded on a school trip for telling the girls who shared a room with her horrible things in the dark about witches who would devour them all. It was no wonder she'd gone on to study library science.

"Are we close?" I asked.

Hours had passed. I had the feeling I was treading an endless path. My left knee hurt.

"We're just at the woods," she said. "Don't rush. We'll get there in time."

We didn't stop once to rest. The rain was running down my face. My back was wet from the water streaming down my neck. The wind was so intense that at one point I had to hug a tree trunk to keep from blowing away.

"It's not dark yet."

"How much time do we have?" I asked.

"Enough," Marija said.

I grabbed the auxiliary rope wherever there was any. It was soaked through. I was afraid it would slip from my hands. I felt exhausted, but I didn't give up. By some miracle I never stumbled. God was watching over me.

I couldn't recall how the landscape looked. I strained to remember, but the image wouldn't come. Out of sight, out of mind. I wanted to ask my sister to describe our surroundings, but I was too ashamed.

The longer we trekked, the more strenuous it became. I was terribly hungry and thirsty. I wanted to lie down and die at the halfway point, but I kept going. Not even a half hour later, all sound disappeared—as if someone had flipped a switch. I'd lost my hearing. My mouth was dry, and I wanted to ask for water, but my sister dragged me by the rope like I was a sack of potatoes and not a human being. I

51

longed to pray, but I had no voice. My knees ached; my arms were bruised. Klek was slowly killing me with its steepness and its slippery rocks. It wanted to churn my immortal soul into humus. Just as I was making peace with death, we arrived at a clearing, probably the peak my sister had read about in the car.

If Marija said something, I didn't hear her. I could only imagine her eagerly announcing to me:

We're here!

or

Finally!

I was blind and deaf, chilled and soaked to the bone. I sat on the ground and began to cry. I'd come to regain my sight and instead lost my hearing.

"There is no God," I said.

As soon as the words left my mouth, I felt a multitude of hands on me. Slowly they removed my helmet, my jacket, then my hiking boots one by one—but they didn't stop there. They completely undressed me. My sweater and pants were torn. My T-shirt too. All that was left was my underwear, and then very gently, just one pair of hands peeled off my panties and bra. I wasn't shivering, even though it was a cold April and the storm had drenched us. To my surprise I was not ashamed, in spite of all the hands on me, not just that one pair, but as many as I could imagine. It was as if there were hundreds of them, covering every part of my naked body. They rubbed heat into me. Then they abruptly withdrew and were replaced by tongues, and then teeth that nibbled on my neck, breasts, abdomen, and clitoris. Passionate little bites that I began to dread. If Jesus had fallen off the wall that first time, what was going to happen now? Would the whole of Croatia fall? The Christian world? Fingers, tongues, and teeth sought to destroy me and civilization, or so I thought—but I soon lost my train of thought. I was only skin, stretched taut by pleasure, like a drum. I didn't need any senses except touch. I came, finally hearing my own voice again as it broke through the sky. But I was still blind.

"Can you hear me?" my sister asked.

"Yes."

My voice was trembling.

"Did you bring a male sacrifice?" I heard unfamiliar female voices ask.

There were a lot of them. They giggled.

"We did," said my sister.

I had no idea what she was talking about.

"Here!" she said.

"What is this?" one of them asked. "It looks very old."

"The finger of Stjepan Tomašević," Marija replied. "You didn't say the victim had to be fresh. Just that it had to be part of a man's body, taken without his consent."

Someone started a bonfire nearby.

"We approve," the smiling voices said. "A sacrifice is a sacrifice."

I felt someone hug me. It was Marija.

"Don't be scared," she said. "When the fire is hot enough, they'll throw the finger in it first and then you. If the fire accepts the male sacrifice, then you'll emerge able to see again."

"And if the fire doesn't accept it?" I was worried.

"You'll die happy," my sister said.

I listened to the women's frenzy. And they eavesdropped on us. Apparently they liked our conversation because a few of them approached. They embraced us and said that sisters never burn.

"But I believe in God!" I shouted with pride.

"That's your problem," they said.

I crouched down. Of everything in this world, I would miss only plants.

"It's time," I heard someone say.

They threw the finger bone into the flames and pushed me in after it.

When I came out, Marija ran up and hugged me tightly. She cried as if she'd pulled me out of a coffin alive. I was silent. I was thinking of Stjepan Tomašević. Now that my sight was restored, I wanted to see if the slain king really was as small as my sister had said.

Fellow's Gully

1

Our phone wouldn't stop ringing. At the time of
that first call, I was going through a phase of not
leaving my bed. I didn't even leave the house for a
week, and didn't change my clothes—I mostly just
wore a blanket over my head. In the half-light I
thought of nothing. I was waiting for life to pass.
My husband tried to rouse me with unappealing
invitations to concerts and movies, but I wasn't
in the mood to socialize. Over those seven days
I brushed my teeth only a few times, and didn't
wash my face once. Occasionally I'd pretend to read
something, but I just gazed through the letters,
through the paper, even through my husband,
who sat at the kitchen table, always with his
back turned.

The phone's ringing surprised us because it was late on a Sunday night. No one ever called at that hour. I could barely rouse myself from bed to answer.

"Good evening." I heard a woman's voice. "Forgive me for calling so late, but I'd like to buy a plot of land from you. The land known as Fellow's Gully. The terrain is quite sloped, and it has a well and a little black locust tree. I'd pay for it immediately, in cash."

The woman did not introduce herself or confirm that she'd called the right number.

"Fellow's Gully? Where's that?" I asked.

"I'm sure you know," she said.

"I think you have the wrong number."

"I don't," she said. "I'll call you again in a week, at the same time. Goodbye."

She'd left me a little dizzy. My husband, confused, looked at me questioningly.

"Fellow's Gully?" he said. "Let's look into it."

Of course, just as I'd thought, neither he nor I owned any land by that name. We inquired, but found nothing. More than a month passed, and the phone stayed silent. I'd almost forgotten the anonymous caller when someone from the cadastre suddenly called to say they'd made a mistake. Some relative had in fact bequeathed my husband the parcel of land called Fellow's Gully in Bilogora.

"Which relative?" he asked.

They said a name he'd never heard before.

"Godek? There's no one in my family with that name."

The land was, by all official accounts, his, but no one had ever called him about a probate hearing. Along with the documents he subsequently had to sign, he received a small photo glued to a piece of cardboard. Beneath the photo someone had written in small letters: *View of house of I. Godek, Bilogora*. They also gave him a small notebook with a tattered green cover that had belonged to his alleged relative, a forestry engineer named Ivo Godek.

Two days later, the anonymous woman called again.

"So will you sell me Fellow's Gully?"

She didn't mention the house in the photo. Perhaps she didn't know about it.

"We need to think it over," I said. "We haven't even seen the land."

It struck me as odd that she knew about the Gully before we did, but I didn't want to tell her that. I thought maybe she worked at the cadastre or the court, and so had some kind of insight into the land registers and related documents.

"If you want to see it," said the woman, "go toward the end of October. That's when the light falls best."

"Falls on what?" I asked.

But the woman had already hung up.

"Something about this isn't right," I grumbled to my husband.

He agreed with me. It seemed like that land would only cause us problems. Still, I was interested to know what Fellow's Gully looked like, and where the picture had come from.

In the photo you could see a country house hidden behind a wooden fence and half-used bales of hay. Above the Bilogora hills, in the background, gathered clouds. The direction of the light wasn't discernible. The road was muddy, the trees bare. I gazed at the photo for a long time. It was immediately clear that it had been taken in the fall, but I couldn't tell if it was October. I wanted to connect the light falling on Fellow's Gully with the photo of the country house. I sensed the call from the woman was no coincidence; neither was this place coincidentally linked to us. I checked out the surname Godek. It was Polish and meant both "reconciliation" and "glory." I was surprised by how disinterested my husband ultimately was. As if the land had nothing to do with him. When I told him I wanted to go see the plot of land before selling it, he didn't want to join me.

"It'll be October soon," I said, indignant. "Doesn't Fellow's Gully interest you at all?"

"It'll interest me when we cash in."

Money hadn't even crossed my mind. For days I couldn't sleep. I imagined what the land looked like in real life: the trees, the well. The whole of September I lay in a stupor.

At the end of October, I got in the car and set

off. Near Fellow's Gully there were a few houses, mostly abandoned, but I managed to find a person who could show me where the parcel was.

"Here we are," said the villager. "Your land stretches from this fence until the other side where the grass is mowed. This overgrown part is Fellow's Gully."

The parcel wasn't small, but it looked that way from being hemmed in by the landscape. The surrounding area was cultivated—only the Gully was neglected.

"If you need anything, just call," said the man.

Before he could get away, I asked, "And Godek's house?"

"Whose house?" he asked, puzzled.

I showed him the picture.

"There's never been a Godek here, or a house."

Once he left, I stepped onto the plot of land hunched over, like I was sitting at a desk rather than walking in nature. My back hurt and I wanted to return to bed as soon as possible. The pain was becoming unbearable. As I waded deeper into the trees and shrubs it only got worse. In the middle of Fellow's Gully there was a small clearing. By the time I reached it my arms were completely scratched up. I looked to see if there was somewhere I could rest. I didn't see any well. I wanted to call my husband, but I had no signal. Finally I took off my jacket, tossed it on the ground, and sat leaning against a locust tree.

I'd almost forgotten Godek the engineer's note-book. My husband had shoved it into my desk drawer along with the other papers. I hadn't gotten a chance to see what was written inside before I made the trip.

The pain in my spine was intensifying, as if the whole piece of land had been dumped on my back. I grabbed the notebook from the inside pocket of my jacket. The first half of it was blank. In the second half, Godek had twice scribbled, in a minuscule hand, interpretations of some old law, and then after that he'd started a "fiscal diary." Income on one side, expenses on the other. I tried to decipher his notes. Right away I recognized some words—*head of section*, *Ministry of Finance*, *construction*, *removal costs*, *surveying*—and then I came to a sentence that totally perplexed me: *This can be (. . .) according to Art. 86 laws governing souls*. Godek must have been confused because I guessed it was supposed to say *soils*, but no, it really said *souls*. The more I peered at the word, the clearer it became to me that this was not an error. Godek had spelled the word correctly.

The fiscal diary noted various expenses and debtors, but I only gave them a cursory glance. A stream of amounts that didn't tell me very much. I barely managed to get up. I wanted to circle the parcel again and try to find the well before heading home. As soon as I walked away from the tree and stepped back into the undergrowth, I felt a loud buzzing in my ears. It didn't stop, even when I got back in the car. The buzzing accompanied me to Zagreb.

I FOUND MY husband sitting at the kitchen table and nervously rubbing his eyes. When he looked at me, one of them was bloodshot.

"Are your allergies bothering you again?" I asked.

The drops he used didn't help. Eventually we both got into bed to try to rest. I didn't know how to start a conversation about Fellow's Gully. My husband showed no interest whatsoever. I cast a sidelong glance in his direction. His face was distorted; he seemed like a stranger who just happened to be in bed beside me. He lay still with his eyes closed, breathing deeply. Lately I'd been absent next to him, engulfed in my own thoughts. Both of us, really, were equally withdrawn, but my discontent became almost tangible and wedged itself between us. I reassured myself that I'd always been this way, but that was a lie. I couldn't remember when sadness had begun to overwhelm me.

"The land we're selling, I'm not sure why the woman who called us wants it. The parcel is completely overgrown. It's just a mess."

My husband was silent. Occasionally he rubbed his irritated eye.

"I wasn't able to find the well. My back was

killing me, so I couldn't stay very long. Maybe you could come with me—that way we could figure out what this is all about together."

"I don't feel like going to that village. I have no idea where this land even came from," he said.

"Maybe it would be best to . . . I'd like to . . ."

Before I could get a complete thought out, the phone rang. Its sound was more penetrating, as if someone had amplified the ringer.

"Hello!" I heard a familiar woman's voice. "Have you been to see the land?"

"I have. There's nothing there. Not even the well you mentioned."

"Surely the well is there. When can we meet?"

"I need to go again with the surveyor," I lied.

I didn't want to sell the land. I don't know why, but I couldn't part with it.

"Why do you even want Fellow's Gully?" I asked.

"For sentimental reasons," the woman said brusquely.

She wouldn't elaborate.

"Could you leave me your name and number so I can contact you?" I asked.

"I'll call you," she said, then hung up.

NATURALLY, I dreamed about Fellow's Gully. In my dream I found the well with no trouble. It was covered with sheet metal, and someone had placed heavy stones on top to keep it in place. The dream was recurring, and every time I'd wake up from it with a mild case of tinnitus. I'd always open my eyes at the same moment—after reaching out my hand to remove one of the stones.

A month later, my husband complained that he couldn't fall asleep at night because his heart was racing. The ceaseless noise of his bloodstream was torturing him. He was aware at every moment of his own life and it drove him crazy. Then he also started experiencing tinnitus. He stayed up all night and was worn to exhaustion. He had all the tests done—spinal X-ray, carotid ultrasound, MRI—but the results came back normal. The buzzing would come out of nowhere.

"Other people can relax because they're not aware of being alive all the time, but my vital signs keep me constantly on edge."

I couldn't quite understand what he was talking about, but as my tinnitus intensified, I began to grasp his problem: my head was a shell with an immense river roaring inside. But I didn't complain about it; his eye was still bloodshot and I didn't want to bother him. We were both stuck in our own anxieties, unable to voice them.

When the phone rang the next time, I didn't answer.

"I don't want to sell the land," I told my husband.

"Why not?" he asked.

"I can't explain why, but please listen to me."

"Okay."

I realized, hugging my husband, that Fellow's Gully had sentimental value for me, too, and I couldn't detach myself from it.

2

The phone wouldn't stop ringing, every night at the same time. I didn't answer it, but I didn't have the strength to cancel the line either. I knew the sound of the ringer would torment me even if I pulled the phone out of the wall. Just before the beginning of winter I told my husband, who still refused to accompany me, that it was time to go to Fellow's Gully again and search for the well.

I was making my way through the locust trees. It was noticeably colder now and my teeth were chattering. I hadn't considered that the temperature would fall as I moved deeper into the land's interior. Although there was no water in sight, my face could feel the proximity of a river cooling the air. Eventually I paused to catch my breath. The tinnitus was killing me, as if someone were shrieking in my ear. I was disoriented. It was thundering in my head.

I looked around a few times, then stood still, feeling lost. It was getting even colder. I'd put on warm boots, but they didn't help at all. The cold was penetrating the ground and every step I took was heavy, as if I were sinking into deep snow, though none had fallen yet. And then I saw something that was not a well at all, but the most ordinary hole in the ground.

MY HUSBAND USED to say that he would often dream of a threadbare mattress on the floor. In his dream he would be sleeping on it and then realize, upon awakening in the dream, that a snake had slithered into the mattress and laid eggs there. I told him we all have nightmares; he assured me, however, that this was no mere nightmare, but rather a dream that had the quality of a memory. We argued about it constantly, never arriving at a resolution. He was convinced he was remembering something that had actually happened, and I kept trying to persuade him that it was just a bad dream.

"When have you ever slept on an old, shabby mattress, let alone one full of snakes?" I asked him.

"I don't know."

I peered down into the hole, or rather into the fissured ground. In the darkness I could make out a flight of steep stairs. I wasn't afraid. I turned on the flashlight on my cell phone (which, oddly, the unknown woman had never called) and gradually descended into the hole. The air felt damp and I was freezing, but curiosity pulled me deeper into the earth. I crept along for some time, slowly so as not to stumble and plummet into the abyss. The sound of roaring water reached my ears. Still climbing down, I looked at my phone and saw that it had already been twenty minutes since I'd entered the hole. Step by step, I finally reached the bottom. There was a light flickering nearby and I headed toward it. The closer I got to the light, the clearer it became that there was a house—in fact, it was Godek's house from the photograph. Though this one was surrounded by complete darkness, there was no mistaking it. My phone's flashlight went out, but I was still able to see. The bales of hay stood in the same place, as did the fence. Only the background was different: the hills of Bilogora were nowhere in sight. Instead of slopes, a huge river flowed in the dark behind the house. It seemed as wide as the Yellow River.

I took in the bleak landscape all around me, determined to continue until I'd made it to the light and the house. I gave the door a firm knock. Once, twice, and then I heard a familiar woman's voice.

"Come in," she said.

She was expecting me. She registered no surprise when I stepped inside. She was lounging in an old, tattered armchair. At one end of the room, I noticed the mattress my husband had told me about: it was on the floor, stained and torn, pushed into a corner.

"I called you," she said, "but you didn't pick up."

"The phone's broken," I lied. "It doesn't ring."

The woman laughed.

"Winter's nearly here," she said. "It's time to say goodbye to your husband and let him come home. That was the deal."

"I don't remember any deal."

"Sit down," she said, pointing to the stool next to her feet.

I obeyed, but first used my foot to inch it closer to the door. I didn't want to sit too close to her. Once I settled, I saw that on the coffee table to her left there was a bowl of pomegranates and figs. A pomegranate lay cracked open in her lap. Its seeds were scattered on the floor. To her right, a small fire was smoldering, so it wasn't that cold, but my teeth were still chattering from the walk.

"We said nine months with you, three months with me."

"I don't remember any deal," I repeated.

"Don't be stubborn," she said, a note of reproach in her voice. "Every year you do this. Don't keep him; there's a lot of work awaiting him here."

I was silent, which annoyed the woman even more.

"Are his eyes already bloodshot? The longer he's up there with you, the harder it'll be for him."

"Just one eye," I said triumphantly.

"Have some pomegranate," she said.

I hesitated, but by now I was so hungry I had to eat something. As soon as I ate the first seed, I remembered why I was there, why every year I ceremonially descended the stairs into the darkness to have a conversation with this woman.

"No!" I shouted, but it was too late.

My husband had to return to the hole, to the dirty mattress, to the underworld every year. The entrance was always in a different place; this year it was Fellow's Gully. I cried, of course, because I could now hear the distorted strains of the lyre and the guitar; the love song I'd composed for my husband was slowly becoming his mother's funeral dirge. The woman eyed me intently. His three months with her felt like an eternity for me above.

Godek was, of course, a pseudonym, because my husband had neither been an engineer nor worked in forestry. All those souls he'd recorded and erased in his notebook had been waiting for nine months in hangars not far from home for my husband to return and settle accounts with them. For three months he lay on the mattress, next to the fire, beneath his mother's feet. He would arise after torturous dreams, go behind the house, and write and erase the names of the dead. When spring arrived, I'd come for him, exhausted by the seasonal depression I'd fallen into during his absence. Sometimes I grew melancholic even sooner; while lulled into a sweet oblivion with him I only foresaw our parting and his return to the underworld, to his mother.

"Take it," she said, pushing the pomegranate into my hands. "As soon as you get home, give it to him to eat."

"All right," I said, but I did not want my husband to remember.

My tongue was heavy; I couldn't speak another word. I stared at the floor in front of me. The tinnitus had stopped, but now my ears were tormented by other sounds: the moaning of the people from the hangars, and the river that would swallow them all, one by one.

I rolled the pomegranate around in my hands, prolonging my departure to the surface.

"Go," the woman said. "You don't have much time."

Outside the house, I looked around once more. The mother's love for her son was a bare landscape, dreary and hostile. I despised this place, and I despised motherhood because it, more than anything else, personified death. Every year my husband died for three months to make his mother feel alive. I spat out the unchewed pomegranate and left Hades as fast as I could.

I immediately felt better out in the fresh air, and my eyes adjusted to the sunlight, but my heart was pounding. I wasn't ready to be separated from my husband. I stood beside that gaping hole in the earth that had birthed him. I felt helpless.

WHEN I SAW my husband for the first time, it was near the river. Across the street from the Croatian national broadcasting headquarters was a series of small gardens whose narrow paths I would walk in the moonlight while others slept. I loved the Sun, of course, but sometimes I could only love nature in the dark. I'd been walking that night to get some air, when I heard the sound of twigs snapping. Curious, I moved toward it to see what was going on and beheld a young man cautiously peeking out of a hole in the ground. He was beautiful. That was what mattered to me most then.

Spring, my season in every sense, always aroused a fierce passion in me. I'd never been overly chaste, but at that moment my thoughts were flooded with the most perverse images. Sometimes out in the gazebo I pretended that I could observe lovers through their bedroom windows, or I crawled along the branches like a nuthatch for a bird's-eye view of the intimacies unfolding in highrises. That evening, when I first saw my husband, I'd been planning to go to an apartment building in the Cvjetno neighborhood where a young couple who exclusively practiced anal sex lived. They had an established routine: they always used almond oil as a lubricant, which excited me, and they never varied their pleasure—always the same positions, the same sounds, the same climax. I'd fallen in love with them. Maybe some of my infatuation transferred to that hole in the ground and spawned a partner with whom I'd be forced to live out a routine of my own: an endless cycle of loving him and then suffering due to his mother. Our relationship was difficult, sometimes painful, and I couldn't help but think that we'd started the cycle that very night when I'd been wanting to watch the young Zagreb couple have anal sex.

After I pulled the young man out of the ground, I immediately brought him home to talk about that unfortunate hole and what had driven him out of it.

"I wanted to see what life was like up above," he said. "To get away from my mother."

At the first mention of his mother, I should've taken him back to where he'd come from, but I was too turned on. I wanted him ferociously and there was no stopping my hunger. I seduced him and penetrated him that night. We fell in love and decided to stay together.

After that, his relationship with his mother was never the same. She tricked us both by feeding us a pomegranate, and that is why her only son was forced to fulfill his role as god of the underworld for three months each year, even though he was ill-suited for the job. Regardless of their deeds, he cast the souls of the dead downstream or upstream—the choice was his mother's alone. He had no autonomy. He emerged from the hole only to reluctantly return to it.

"If this is motherhood," I told him, "I never want to be a mother."

WHEN I GOT back to Zagreb, I recounted to my husband everything that had happened at Fellow's Gully.

"We need to get rid of your mother," I said.

"Impossible," he said. "No matter what, I still love her."

He ate the pomegranate and his memory was restored. He looked awful, as if at death's door. I gazed at him, and after weeks of having no libido at all, I was seized by arousal. As if my descent into the underworld had revived my desire. I called him Mr. Godek, first as a joke, and then compulsively, convinced that the role suited him and it was time for him to come inside me.

The next evening, he started packing. I refused to help him; I couldn't move, and the discomfort his departure always caused me made it even harder. I looked at a drop of his semen on my fingertip and imagined it as a spark that could burn the entire underworld and incinerate his mother. The vilest thoughts were spinning in my head, but I was not ashamed of them.

"Maybe," I said, "maybe . . . your mother can't swim."

"She can swim," he said. "Remember how I tried to push her into the water when I was a boy? She just walked on the surface."

"What are you thinking about right now?" I asked, nervous.

"The mattress that's waiting for me—it's disgusting."

"A symbol of the deepest maternal love," I snapped.

"Maybe."

I drove him to Fellow's Gully, he climbed down into the hole, and the ground closed up behind him. I'd effectively buried my husband. We hadn't even kissed goodbye. He hadn't looked back. I couldn't tell if his hurried footsteps were a sign that he was terrified of seeing his mother or secretly looking forward to their reunion. Just like at every other departure, he'd hurt me.

The first thing I did as a widow—in the form of a bird, free—was fly to my own mother, to complain about my mother-in-law. She hugged me and said, "It's high time you looked for a new husband."

I agreed, even though I still loved him. The earth didn't simply open up every day to toss a handsome, eager young man into my arms. He was now neatly buried in the possessive embrace of his mother and her sick, suffocating love. Just as a drop of his semen had briefly illuminated my path, so, too, did it serve as a beacon for his mother in the deepest dark of hell. I felt sorry for them both at that moment, but even in winter, life had to go on. That night I crept into the desolate gardens near the river, looking absently for cracks in the hardened earth. I loved my mother, but I needed a weaker love, something that wouldn't last a lifetime.

1740

I'M SITTING ON my front patio. Drenched in sweat.
The last time Vilko came by, he left me some deodorant and insect repellant, but I use both sparingly.
The sweat from my armpits reminds me of the literature I read to make the days seem shorter. Sappy
romance novels, occasionally Dostoevsky (which
causes me to sweat from discomfort), and rarely,
when I can summon the strength, natural history,
stories about animals, about bygone eras and
extinct species. Those books make me sweat the
most, but I pretend it's from the heat and humid-
ity. I even pretend for Vilko, and I've known him for
years. While she was still alive, my mother used to
say she had no time for books because there were
better things to do. As a result, I didn't like reading either, but now I have all the time in the world.
I need to spend it somehow.

Humans aren't exactly an extinct species from the distant past, but they're endangered by their efforts to survive at all costs. People can survive anything and everything, but if I were to spend all day making a list of what's survivable, I'd probably die from sheer agony. Instead I stick my head in books and pretend that, in moments like these, stories make sense. I don't want to brood, so I read. I devour words. A little drop of sweat trickles down my cheek. I say it's a drop of sweat, but of course I'm lying. Lying helps me survive—it's because of lying that I'm not an extinct species myself. I've been lying my entire life. I don't know exactly what I'm reading—a historical lie, descriptions of some past era's glorious prosperity, something about the Western Roman Empire. Petronius's *Satyricon*? The letters look blurry; I'm sweating so much I can no longer see them clearly. Fat drops fall onto the paper. I wipe my eyes with a cloth from the side table.

Before I can continue reading, I hear the sound of a motor—it's Vilko's boat making its way to my house. No one else visits me, only Vilko and sometimes Višnja, his wife. He tries to persuade me to take my boat over to their place in the center of Zagreb, but I'm a rat who jumped ship to survive. The floods drove me away to my cabin. Once in a while I go to the city to buy supplies, but then I quickly retreat home, to continue wasting my life with literature as much as I possibly can. I mostly lounge on the patio, which gives me a view of the other cabins and the garbage dump close to our neighborhood. No one bothers to cover the garbage anymore because the water carries it away regardless. Right now, there's a rainbow over the dump. I stare at it. I need to look at something to calm my nerves.

Vilko approaches from the left, but I keep staring straight ahead. I throw the dirty, damp cloth on the floor. I don't throw it, really, I drop it, but I like to pretend I'm doing things consciously, making an effort. When Vilko cuts the motor, I can hear the waves lapping lightly against the improvised dock where he quickly ties up the boat. From the corner of my eye, I can see that he's carrying a crate, but I don't get up to help him. I don't go to greet him. I hate people, even those I consider friends. Vilko hastily climbs onto the patio.

"You're crying again?" he asks.

He never beats around the bush. Maybe that's why I still consider him a friend.

"It's sweat," I lie. "It's hot."

I have a headache. Vilko rests the crate at my feet. Inside there's a loaf of bread, a bit of lard, some milk. Underneath there's something else, but I don't lift the kitchen towel that Višnja covered the food with for protection from flies. I note only what's visible. What I can count on.

"Višnja says hi," Vilko says.

I'm silent. I'm sure he made that up.

"She couldn't come because she's working, but she made you a cake and some dandelion honey."

"Where'd she find dandelions?" I ask, surprised.

"At the market, from the woman she always buys from."

Humans lie to survive, as I've already stated, but I repeat, they lie and lie, and most of all to themselves. And now Vilko's standing here and lying about where Višnja shops, which has nothing to do with what we used to call a "market." I look at him and quiet my thoughts. I don't want sweat to roll down my cheeks again. My eyes itch and I rub them nervously. I know they're red.

"Don't cry," Vilko says.

His words are never meant to console me, only himself. If my tears flow then his will too: maybe not now, but when he's back in his boat again and heading home, he'll start to cry. He'll admit to himself there's no more market, that Višnja bought the dandelions in a place that bears no resemblance to one. The monoculture farming systems that feed us don't need markets. He's aware of that. If Vilko isn't crying now, it just means that he cried earlier, before he came over.

"Višnja also wanted to give you a book," he says, rummaging through the crate.

He pushes a volume into my hands. I look at what he's given me. Nina Epton, *Love and the French*.

"I have this."

"That's a shame," Vilko says.

"Where'd she get it?" I ask.

"The same woman she bought the dandelions from."

I don't give the book back.

"This one's in better shape than mine. Thank her for me?"

I can see he's glad I'm keeping it.

"She knows you love that topic, and the eighteenth century."

"Višnja knows everything," I say.

Vilko nods, but I'm sure he's bothered by my sarcastic tone. He sits in the chair next to mine, even though I haven't offered it. We're old friends—he doesn't need to ask.

"She also found some books on the history of prostitution, but the covers were water-damaged, so she didn't take them."

"That would be too many books at once."

"I know, but she says you have a lot of catching up to do since you didn't read before the warming."

"As I said, your Višnja knows everything."

I've purposely thrown in *your* to see how Vilko will react, but nothing. We sit in silence. I look at his and Višnja's boat. They've renamed it again. First, they wrote *Višnja* on it, but then they repainted it and wrote *Albertina*. Now it just says *Boat*.

"You can't decide on a name?"

"*Albertina* was a nice name, but I wasn't sure this clunker deserved it."

"But *Boat*?"

"That was Višnja's idea."

"Of course," I say.

"You know her sense of humor."

"It's always been terrible."

We stare at the garbage dump. I know we can't spend the whole time talking about Višnja. It remains to be seen which of us will have the guts to bring up the real reason for Vilko's visit. After all, I can go out for food on my own. This is about something bigger, something much more important. Vilko's leg is furiously shaking. That always happens when he's nervous. He needs time to gather his thoughts. I'm expecting some grievance, but he surprises me. His voice is excited, almost joyful.

"I think we're close," he says. "Just a couple more weeks and the machine will be finished."

"Are you joking?"

"Višnja worked on the program all night. That's why she didn't come with me. Fink and Gmaz are with her. We're almost there."

"Are you sure?" I can't believe my ears.

"The code you rewrote works."

I don't know what to say. I recall the lines I wrote on a piece of greasy paper that Višnja had used to wrap a slab of bacon. My strokes were a sort of calligraphy, but those lines of code, casually recorded, were like the name *Albertina*: pretty, but completely inappropriate for the situation in which we've found ourselves. I don't know where

I got the inspiration. I hardly ever turn on the computer these days. I didn't want to spend all my time staring at the program Gmaz and Višnja had written. It struck me as crude, in the same way the flooded Balkans did: pearls scattered among the fetid, trash-filled water. I peer at that water now, stunned. I don't know what I'm feeling. The floods and the computer program both are the product of human hands. How can we make such lovely and such disgusting things at the same time?

Vilko doesn't push me to speak. He knows I'm in shock. I've fixed my gaze on the red buoy that a relative of mine sent me along with a fishing net, fishing rod, and some bait. The water is higher than ever before, and I often awake in terror from its murmur. I fear the water level will quietly rise until all of us drown in our sleep. The question is whether I managed to fix Gmaz's part of the code because I was terrified, as I first claimed to Višnja, or because I wanted to regain a false sense of control. I stare at the buoy and the water as if I'm seeing far into the future. I avoid my reflection: the only thing more horrible than the flooding is the human face. My thoughts wander and I don't know what to say. I don't want to contemplate Vilko's words. They're too significant. I think instead about how I never used to enjoy going to the sea, and now it comes right up to my doorstep. And I can't even fish—there are almost no more fish left. The fishing gear flung on the patio only serves as a reminder. There's no point in throwing it away though because I know everything I discard will float right back. People can no longer hide their mistakes anywhere.

"I didn't think it would work," I say to Vilko after the long silence. "I was convinced it wouldn't."

Before the flooding, I worked with Višnja and Vilko at the Ruđer Bošković Institute. I was a theoretical physicist, but I also did programming on the side because my parents loved money and wanted me to love it just as much.

You're too prone to abstraction, my mother said.

She wanted me to study economics and management.

The money's in the money, she added.

My father agreed.

As long as she doesn't study the humanities, my mother declared to the family while making rakija.

Traditional values had always mattered in the Balkans, and my parents were no exception. Family, money, and rakija. Rakija was always made at our house, at the cabin where, after the warming, I was ultimately forced to live alone. I've often thought about our long-lost fruit trees. Plum, pear, apple. And especially the cherry tree. Sitting on this patio, I drank the entire supply of rakija my parents had stored in the attic for my future wedding, out of my mind with fear of drowning. One can still find potable water, but there's no more rakija. My parents come to mind from time to time, but alcohol is there constantly. In truth, the memory of rakija compelled me, sweaty and tired as I was, to write code on that greasy paper. I've missed it something awful. The cemetery where my parents are buried is underwater. The Balkans are underwater. The only thing keeping me from drowning is the memory of višnjevača, the rakija that's sweet and tart all at once, like life, like humanity. If the rakija is good, you never get a headache. I want to drink, forget everything, if only for a moment. I stare at the garbage dump day in, day out. I stare at the consequences. I want to get away from them.

"How many of us can fit in the machine?" I ask Vilko.

"All five of us. Fink and Gmaz can sit in the back."

"There wasn't enough room for everyone before."

"I know," Vilko replies. "But Višnja moved the controls and took out a panel we didn't need. If they squeeze in, they can both fit."

"And me?"

"There's always been space for you."

"Are you sure?" I ask.

Vilko looks at me. He senses my apprehension.

"Višnja won't have a problem with it. You helped her a lot with the code."

"I know, but . . ."

"No 'buts,'" says Vilko.

"There's always a 'but,'" I correct him. "Especially with Višnja."

I drank the last bit of rakija two years ago. I

scoured the attic in hopes of finding a stray bottle, one that had perhaps rolled under my mother's old furniture, but there was nothing. Višnja and Vilko never drank—they wanted to be fully present, sober witnesses to the demise of the human race. They were far nobler people than I was. Science was supposed to be noble, but the ideas I worked on were so abstract that nobility didn't matter that much. Ideas simply existed. The idea of progress, for example. I'd always been in favor of progress. Exactly what kind of progress wasn't important. I just wanted to move forward. I didn't care about money quite as much as my parents wanted me to, but I loved having it all the same because money and progress were closely related. All of my abstract ideas were constrained by the reality of money.

I failed as a scientist but succeeded as a programmer. I made money for others, and then for myself. I purchased real estate, invested in various funds and companies. I ultimately accumulated so much money that Vilko and Višnja couldn't even imagine my net worth. That money wasn't earned through science, but it helped raise the air temperature by one and a half degrees Celsius, which ruined my life. What had appeared abstract to people became very concrete when it began to affect their lives.

When it began to affect your *life*, Višnja would correct me.

"I remember," I say to Vilko absentmindedly, "the cherry tree my parents had in front of the house. Its blossoms were so beautiful, thanks to my father's diligent care. I miss that tree the most."

Vilko has heard this story so many times he knows it by heart, but he doesn't interrupt me. He can tell I'm falling into one of my inevitable nostalgic moods.

"It's hard to imagine it was there, just a few steps away from us. And look now!"

I gesture toward the garbage dump.

"Look!"

"I'm looking," Vilko says, but he isn't.

Višnja was rather touched the first time I told her about my father and the tree, presumably because of the relation to her name, which means "cherry," but then she realized I was secretly drinking rakija and stopped coming to listen to my laments about better times.

You don't care about the consequences of global warming, she once said angrily. *You're just sorry you can't drink yourself into oblivion with this swamp water we're surrounded by.*

I didn't contradict her. After that, Vilko started visiting on his own. He kept me apprised of their progress in constructing the machine. I didn't resent Višnja. She rarely came by, only when she needed to ask me about some complicated detail. She'd consult me, I'd help her, but she never stuck around. Not like Vilko, sitting on the patio and watching the rainbow over the dump. Višnja had never been particularly sentimental. It was clear she'd never seek solace in alcohol. She couldn't understand me.

"It's still unbelievable to me," says Vilko, "that you managed to solve our biggest puzzle with a magic marker on greasy paper."

I told everyone I'd had a sudden burst of inspiration, but that, of course, was a lie. I'd in fact spent the entire day at the computer, chewing on my lower lip. I'd tinkered with Višnja and Gmaz's code, which Vilko had brought me with the insect repellant and deodorant. I saw the outline of Višnja's idea. I could clearly grasp what she had in mind, even though she'd mentioned it only in passing. She never wanted to show me the whole program; she'd brought only the tricky parts she needed help with. She didn't trust me. I'd just barely managed to persuade Vilko to copy the rest and bring it without Višnja's knowledge.

"I'm not sure that's a good idea," he had said at first.

"Of course it isn't, but you need my help."

He knew I was right. Fink and Vilko were engineers. Gmaz was a programmer, but he was incompetent. Višnja did anything and everything.

"You don't have to tell her right away," I insisted to Vilko.

"I do have to tell her; I never lie to her. Never."

"Fine, but tell her when I've finished the code."

In the end he showed me sketches of the machine. Half of the construction had been done at the institute, in secret, and the other half in Višnja's garage. That half had been made of parts stolen from experimental monuments and sculptures by Vojin Bakić.

"If they catch you destroying a Bakić, you'll be out of a job. Both of you," I said.

"His work has been destroyed before. They took the plaque from his monument at Petrova Gora, but nothing happened."

"That was before," I said. "Times are different now."

"We stole them for the greater good," Vilko said, attempting to justify himself.

For the greater good is such a tired phrase. Virtue, the greater good—stupid notions that even the literature I've been devouring of late doesn't portray as particularly wise or inspiring. Goodness is overrated. Especially in the sciences. What I was feeling, on the other hand, was not a cliché. I wanted to write the program to completion, my way, then hop into the machine and finally escape. My feelings deserved the trip that Višnja so selfishly wanted for herself and her friends alone.

"I'm giving you twenty-four hours," said Vilko, "and then I'm telling her. Don't screw me over."

"I won't," I promised.

Whenever I felt very sad, and Vilko was nowhere in sight, I'd sit in my boat and ride around the settlement. The majority of my neighbors had left this area around Zagreb. I didn't know where they'd gone. A few remained. They'd been good friends of my late parents. Before the warming, everyone had grown identical gardens and orchards. They'd celebrated Christmas and Easter together. Eaten turkey and mlinci flatbread. Some of them had made bad wine, some honey, but most prepared homemade rakija in large pots. If there was anything the neighbors remembered my parents by, it was their rakija. And my mother's bragging about how smart I was for not studying the humanities.

She'll make money, she said.

What my mother didn't know was that I would have money, just not a future. She couldn't connect those two things because she didn't trouble her mind with what wasn't directly in front of her. She couldn't understand that abstract ideas have concrete consequences.

Money is what's heating up the environment, Višnja told my mother, but at that point it was already too late.

Višnja was always right up front at all the protests. When birds began to die off, even the common species we'd taken for granted, she and Vilko were the first to write a letter to the institute demanding that it support the Council of Environmental Protection.

The council needs more funding, they wrote.

I mocked her at work.

Didn't you say that money is the problem? And now you're begging for some?

Don't be cynical, she said.

But (the eternal *but*) I wanted to be a cynic. I was a cynic. It was a conscious decision. My character. I devoted myself to making snide comments to my colleagues and strangers on the internet. I didn't spare my handful of friends. I was my most cynical around them.

"You've gone silent again," Vilko says.

I forgot that I haven't answered him. My mind is racing with thoughts of the machine.

"Where did you put it?"

"Put what?" Vilko asks.

"The machine."

"In the garage. We have to hide it from the institute."

"Can I see it?"

"Now?"

Vilko seems surprised. I've never asked to see it before.

"If it's not a problem, that is. Do you want to check with Višnja?" I ask.

Vilko nervously fumbles in his pocket to retrieve his phone. He calls Višnja. I can't hear what she's saying.

"Višnja says it's too crowded in the garage right now, but you can come tomorrow."

"Perfect," I say.

When Vilko leaves, I get into my boat and follow his. He's distracted and doesn't notice me trailing him. I shut off the motor to be quiet. He doesn't go to the garage or the institute, but rather to Gmaz's house. I recognize the facade. Fink opens the door for him. Before Vilko enters, I see him kick away some garbage that's floated up to the door.

"YOU CAN'T ONLY read literature that makes you cry," Višnja tells me when I see her the next day.

"You're right," I say. "Sometimes I forget how sensitive I am."

"That's your mother's fault."

"You blame her for everything except global warming," I say.

"I wouldn't be wrong to blame her for that too. She laughed when I said she needed to sort her trash."

"She didn't know any better."

"Now her unsorted trash comes up to your cabin to haunt you," says Višnja.

She was in a good mood.

"Thanks for the cake and honey," I say.

"Vilko said you already have the book about love."

"I do, but that's okay."

I don't want to talk about love, only about machines. Specifically one machine. Višnja's machine. As if she knows my thoughts, Višnja purposely avoids the subject and talks about everything else instead. Luckily Gmaz has just returned with parts to install on the steering console. He's hoping to pass quickly through the kitchen, but I ask him a question before he can get away.

"Is that part of the steering console from a motorboat?" I ask.

"Uh-huh," Gmaz says.

Neither he nor Fink is especially talkative. Compared to them, I'm a chatterbox.

"Do you need help with that?"

I want to see the machine, and Višnja's never going to show it to me.

"You're not an engineer," he says.

Višnja doesn't say anything, but I can see her gripping the edge of a chair. I've spoiled her mood.

"Where's Vilko?" she asks Gmaz.

"In the garage," he replies. "Waiting for this part."

Gmaz lifts the console into the air. He holds it above his head long enough for me to make out the model number. I memorize it and follow him into the garage where the others are waiting. Before we're out of sight, I notice Višnja observing me carefully. Just as I've read the steering console, she's been reading me. I feel like a piece of plastic garbage my mother stubbornly refused to sort while she was alive.

In the garage, Fink sits at the computer and meticulously reviews some calculations. Vilko connects wires inside the machine.

"I found it!" Gmaz yells.

"Well done!" Fink says.

Vilko puts out his hand for the console, but Gmaz places it on the worktable.

"Višnja needs to inspect it first. We can't dismantle and install it just yet."

"Good point," says Vilko.

He gets out of the machine and can't hide his surprise at seeing me.

"Višnja knows you're here?"

"We were just chatting in the kitchen."

"Then it's all right," Vilko says.

I sit down next to Fink. I'm interested in what he's doing.

"What are these calculations?" I ask.

He doesn't respond.

"Why are you all being so secretive?"

I want my question to sound playful, but my tone is earnest.

"That was the plan," I hear Višnja's voice behind me.

"You don't trust me?"

I already know the answer. We worked together for years, after all.

"Not one bit," she says.

"You have no reason to doubt me. I've changed. I read books now."

Višnja laughs.

"The warming melted the Arctic, but it'll never thaw your face."

I act as if I haven't heard the insult. Višnja is right. My face looks the same even when I'm crying.

Nothing can soften it. I look like a villain. I know that.

"Blame it on genetics," I say.

"Look at this," Vilko says to Gmaz.

He wants to stop the argument. When I turn my head, Višnja's no longer in the garage. I love bringing up genetics because this is another part of Balkan heritage: genetics, money, and rakija. Whenever Višnja came home with me during college, she found conversation with my parents repulsive. They always brought up the same subjects. When my father claimed I'd inherited my mother's looks and his brains, Višnja rolled her eyes. I never met her parents. I didn't even know where she was from.

Are you even from here? I had asked her.

It doesn't matter, she said.

But it does matter. That's why she hid it.

No one dares to install the console until Višnja returns. I offer to go over the software with Gmaz and review the elements they're unsure about, but they turn me down. I sit there for fifteen minutes in total silence. Even Vilko doesn't speak to me. Finally I get up and leave. Višnja isn't in the kitchen to say goodbye to.

On my way back home, I stop by the house of a neighbor who resells motorboats. I write down the numbers I memorized from Gmaz's console on a piece of paper.

"This'll take a few days," my neighbor says, "but it shouldn't be a problem."

"Thanks," I say.

"Thank you."

The company he founded was doing well even before the flooding and has since become indispensable. He's profited from others' misfortune. I'd invested a lot of money in him. It's paying off.

"ARE YOU OKAY?" Vilko asks me the next time he visits.

We haven't spoken all week.

"I've seen better days," I say.

My neighbor has procured the console and isn't even charging me for it. There's never been a day better than today, but Vilko doesn't need to know that.

"You know Višnja," he says. "She holds grudges."

After I began to earn significant income from programming, Višnja asked me to fund her work at the institute. She wanted to devote herself more fully to research that wasn't lucrative. Ideas too abstract even for theoretical physics often ended up at the bottom of some administrator's filing cabinet. Višnja didn't think in terms of market demand, so she wasn't bringing in enough money for the institute. I could have helped her, but I didn't want to.

"You have to understand that I just didn't believe time travel was possible then," I tell Vilko.

"You don't need to explain," he says.

"Višnja will never let me go with you."

"She will, don't worry."

"She's suspicious," I say.

"She thinks you're going to sabotage us."

"Don't be ridiculous," I say. "No one wants to get out of here more than I do."

"I know, but Višnja believes you don't actually want to help, and that you'll take a valuable spot. We could instead give it to a biologist or some other expert who'd be able to warn the Yugoslav public about global warming."

"All I said to her was that I wasn't sure that anyone in the Communist Party of Yugoslavia would entertain the ideas of time travel and global warming."

"We have to try," says Vilko.

"But why go to 1964, exactly, and why Yugoslavia? Why not the United States? And even a few years later? People didn't even have the internet then."

"The Communists were the avant-garde. Yugoslavia was nonaligned. Višnja's afraid this technology could fall into the wrong hands. She wants to get to Edvard Kardelj and Miroslav Krleža."

"Višnja's a fool!" I scoff.

"There's nothing foolish about her intentions. Don't forget that the machine is partly Bakić's creation. He would be the first to recognize the polyvalent forms he explored and constructed in those years."

"She's looking for an artist to help her fight global warming? Don't make me laugh."

Višnja is by no means a fool. But I would never admit that. Everything Vilko said makes sense, but I have different plans. Now that I've gotten a steering console like the one they're planning to use for the trip, I can finally relax. I sleep better. I no longer have nightmares about drowning. I feel a euphoria that before I only found in a bottle of sweet, syrupy cherry rakija.

"She only wants what's best for us," Vilko says.

"I'm not sure Višnja is the person who should be deciding what's best for me," I say. "I think there are people at the institute who would make a different, more responsible decision."

Vilko gets up suddenly. He understands my threat.

"I told you you're coming with us. This is Višnja's life's work. You can't deny that."

"Tell her I want a place in the time machine. I want to get out of here."

"If you'd read Krleža, you'd understand us better," Vilko says before storming off.

NIGHT HAS ALREADY fallen when Višnja calls me.

"Okay, you can come with us," she says.

Blackmail always works. Even when I'm sober.

The first major floods began in 2014. The levees from the Yugoslav era hadn't been maintained, and people had illegally used backhoes to steal sand from the banks of the Sava River, destroying the shoreline and leaving their houses exposed. Italians had poached protected species of birds with rented guns and smuggled them back across the border. The clear-cutting of forests had intensified. Green spaces had been paved over and the water had no place to go. I remember it perfectly because Višnja would never shut up about what would happen if people didn't act. She'd predicted the catastrophe. Experts around the world had agreed with her, but I'd just buried my father and couldn't have cared less. I don't want to make excuses, but the fact is that we can't always ponder big problems when burdened by private sorrows. My biggest problem was my mother, not global warming. A few years later, Višnja frantically read and recounted the UN's report on carbon dioxide emissions. She sent it to everyone on the institute's mailing list. People began giving her the side-eye. They wanted to earn their cash and vacation on the Adriatic coast. They didn't care to think about the water rising to their front doors. Such an outcome sounded like science fiction.

The Arctic is melting, Višnja told her colleagues. *We're going to lose Dalmatia and Istria. We're going to be left without a coast.*

But what was an iceberg to me when I had a mother to deal with? I carried a flask with my favorite višnjevača to work every day. Theoretical physics wasn't helping, programming wasn't help-ing—I even grew numb to money. Vilko and Višnja took me out for dinner a few times, and paid the check even though I made more than they did. They were good people, but that didn't help either. When I thought about Višnja's time machine, it seemed to me that no place existed in the space-time continuum that could get me far enough away from my problems. Maybe the point of singu-larity would help, I thought as I sipped my rakija. Either way, I didn't want to give Višnja money for her research.

IF I UNDERSTAND Vilko correctly on the phone, we need to set off on the trip to 1964 in three days. Our connection is poor and I have to call him back.

"The computer is causing interference," he says.

I hear noise in the background. Apparently Višnja is testing the console and the emergency brake.

"What should I bring?" I ask.

"Nothing but water," Vilko says.

Over the next three days I finish my own console and test its function with a remote control. The keys work and I practice using them. At the moment when Višnja types in the destination year, I'll quickly reenter her input. I'm not sure if it'll include any kind of authorization code. Actually, I'm sure that it must, because she still doesn't trust me, especially now that I've threatened her. To her mind, the year 1964 means survival, but I don't trust people who don't lie. People who don't lie and scheme don't want to survive at all costs. Višnja has scruples, and as far as I'm concerned, that's her biggest weakness. Survival demands the worst of us. Of course I'm careful not to let Vilko sense that I'm planning something—he'd immediately tell Višnja and the rest of the crew. They still believe science should be noble.

While I'm working on the console I have no time to read, though Vilko's allusion to Krleža has intrigued me. It's too late to find one of his books. Višnja only respects progress with no commercial value, so I assume that this author, this Miroslav Krleža, shares her outlook. I'm not familiar with the other communist Vilko mentioned. Kardelj something, but to me it's not important.

I disassemble my console and put the most important part into a small case I can easily hide up my sleeve. I have a copy of the program Višnja wrote for the time machine on my computer. It isn't hard to modify the design. Despite our troubles with flooding, technology has continued to advance.

"YOU CAN COME now," Vilko says on the phone three days later.

Before I climb into my boat, I look around. I want to remember the future I'm about to irreversibly abandon. Instead of water, I bring the console and a favorite photograph of me and my parents standing in the orchard. To my father's left is the blooming cherry tree, our family's favorite.

When I arrive at the garage, everyone is ready and bursting from excitement. They can't do a test run because they're not certain they can return to the exact same moment they've departed from. The time machine isn't totally reliable in that way, but Višnja claims that the journey through a wormhole in one direction is as real as the reality of global warming. Everyone has absolute faith in her. She knows what she's doing.

"We have only one chance," she says. "Every trip after that will vary randomly by give or take three hundred years. Maybe even more. The coordinates I've inputted are a safety net, but they're no guarantee."

I close my eyes for a moment and imagine space bending at the time machine's command.

"Are you ready?" Višnja asks me.

"Yes," I lie.

Fink and Gmaz sit as Vilko described, at the back of the machine. A piece of a Bakić juts out above their heads. Višnja takes her seat at the steering console. Vilko sits on her right, and I, on her left. I have my back turned to her.

"Testing, one, two, three," she says in a loud voice.

I hear buttons being pressed and the safety switch being activated. I assume she's unlocked the time machine with her thumbprint. Then, on my own miniature console, which I've synchronized with hers, I see that Višnja has typed in *March 1, 1964*. Vilko explains it's important for us to arrive prior to the convening of the Eighth Congress of the League of Communists of Yugoslavia in Belgrade. There the Yugoslav communists will repeal the Five-Year Plan of 1961 to 1965 and announce the "great economic reform" that will open up Yugoslav society to a market economy and capitalism.

"Our problems began in December 1964," he says. "We need to show Kardelj the consequences. He needs to really see them."

He's referring to the high rate of unemployment that followed, but not just that, because in Višnja's mind everything is connected: the free market, economic inequality, inflation, and global warming. She's always seen the big picture. But the picture in the forefront of my mind is my family photograph. We sit huddled together in the time machine, but there are light-years between us. It's impossible to reconcile our ideologies. Vilko's been a fool to try to keep us together. He's been a fool to trust me.

Right before Višnja starts the machine, I input the year 1740 on my console. The change happens so quickly it goes unnoticed. She presses the button that's supposed to take us to Zagreb in 1964.

GMAZ IS THE first to disembark. He vomits, of course, because the machine has wrung us out like wet beach towels. Before he can look up, out jumps Fink, who's tolerated the time travel much better.

"This isn't Zagreb," he says.

He points to Versailles.

"What is that?" Višnja asks, dumbfounded.

"Versailles."

"What year? How did we end up here?" She looks at me. Then she looks down at my hands. She sees the reserve console.

"Idiot!" she screams. "What have you done?"

"I've returned us to a better time. Isn't that what you wanted?"

"What year is this?" Fink asks.

"1740," I say.

Vilko is silent. I know he's consumed by the sweet feeling of guilt.

"This is awful," he says after a moment. "None of us knows French."

"You're wrong," I say cheerfully.

Unlike them, I speak the language fluently.

"I can teach you how to say 'višnja' in French— it's 'cerise,'" I say. "Learn that word well because you're going to need it."

Everyone is visibly upset. They don't even know where to start with eighteenth-century France, but I'm more than ready. We have about fifty years until the revolution, in which Višnja will surely fare well. But now we're on my turf: we've come to the most delightful, most debauched age of Louis XV. I'm looking forward to the outrageous behavior of his courtiers.

"We're in for some sweet cherry-picking," I say.

The eighteenth century promises different rhythms, devoid of consequences I might personally face. Višnja is crying. Seeing her tears, I feel an onrush of pleasant emotions I haven't known in a long time, not since my mother's death.

An earlier version of this story was published in 2019 in *McSweeney's Quarterly Concern: 2040 A.D.*, issue 58.

Mama

IT'S WRONG TO take one's mother from behind,
Ivor read, because whoever dreams of such things
will find himself shunned by his mother, his home-
land, his profession, and everything he cares about.
Ivor lay his head on the desk. The author he was
reading, that damn Artemidorus Daldianus, wrote
in the *Oneirocritica* that "imagining to be given oral
sex by one's mother is most terrible of all," and Ivor
had dreamed of exactly that: his own mother on
her knees. In his dream, he'd repeated his mother's
name like a mantra: Lidija, Lidija, Lidija! He'd awakened with a start, and fortunately hadn't finished.
His humiliation was not complete. Artemidorus had
been writing long before Freud, but his tone was
similarly accusatory: fucking one's own mother
wasn't exactly acceptable behavior in the second
century either. Other people's mothers were fair

game, of course, but yours should be banished from your head. On top of all this, Ivor despised his mother, sometimes so fiercely that he hated himself for it.

Lidija and Ivor had a daily routine: they would stroll together up and down Šaban Zahirović Street. She in her fur coat with her hair coiffed, he with his back slightly hunched, as if he were her servant and not her son. In reality they looked more like a couple. It made him uncomfortable, but he went along with the game because it gratified Lidija to have an obedient son who sprang to attention at her every word and took care not to embarrass her at school or in public. It was important to him to have a mother. He didn't want to anger her with the wild sensibilities of a future writer. He planned to get his revenge in his novels. That was the only reason he put up with her.

For weeks, Ivor had dreamed only of his mother. Had society not already turned its back on him, he would've agonized over Artemidorus's warnings against incestuous dreams. But this was superstitious nonsense, and he felt at ease—nothing could be worse than living with Lidija. He had to comb her hair before bed, massage her legs and feet. Help her get dressed. Bring her tea. Rub her back in the bathtub, even though she wasn't even fifty and was perfectly capable of doing it herself. He wondered when she would start asking him to wipe her ass and change her sanitary pads.

In his room (which had no lock) Ivor was quiet in his sexual exploits. He always ejaculated in toilet paper, quietly, so quietly, and then flushed it. It was critical not to leave the slightest trace of semen, which Lidija could smell like a hunting dog. He feared she would bite his head off and throw him out in the street. So he diligently studied literature, took his mother for walks, dreamed at night about her orally satisfying him—and thus did his days pass. But then the incestuous dreams suddenly stopped. Instead of his mother kneeling before him, there was a woman—well, not a woman, perhaps a girl-creature: she had horns and big doe eyes. His genitals disappeared in her maw, which was big enough to swallow him whole. The girl was a beast, that was clear, but a considerate beast who would tear out his liver and spleen only after she'd left him completely spent. These were happy dreams and Ivor woke up relieved, feeling no remorse for having replaced his mother with a different monster.

Lidija never spoke about Ivor's father.

"He was a drunk—he died the way he lived, like a dog."

Ivor had seen a photo of his father once, quite by accident. He immediately noticed that they looked nothing alike. Ivor didn't look like his mother either. He knew, however, that he wasn't adopted, because Lidija surely would've rubbed his face in such illegitimacy on a daily basis. But she'd never called him a bastard. Sometimes he perceived a look of disgust on her face, but it was accompanied by fear. He couldn't explain it.

His father had evidently died under strange circumstances: he'd gotten drunk and drowned in a shallow, dirty puddle, not even up to his ankles. Ivor would've understood his mother's contempt for him had he been the spitting image of his late father, but nothing on his face recalled the dead man. Maybe Lidija was repulsed by the very act in which he'd been conceived?

Sometimes Ivor wore his mother's clothes, but this was to be expected: he wanted to get inside Lidija's skin, to understand her behavior, her aversion to men and their "degenerate desires." He would put on his mother's bra then her fur coat, and parade around the apartment and in front of the mirror. He would talk to himself, imitating her voice. As soon as Lidija left to meet her friends for coffee, he would take out her jewelry and makeup. He resembled her most when he was wearing makeup. He found comfort in that.

Lidija was reluctant to let him go out, and he had to meet up with people in secret. At the university he had a few good female friends with whom he enthusiastically discussed Byron. They all were in love with him. He wanted his mother to love him, too, at least a little, but she'd finished her literary studies long before. They were lost to each other.

A BIG GAPING mouth. Razor-sharp teeth, dripping with glistening saliva. A black, forked tongue running along Ivor's genitals. He holds her by the horns and fucks her in the muzzle. He looks down and sees his reflection in her eyes. There isn't enough toilet paper in the world to hide his desire for the creature, with her sharp horns and soft palate. He wakes up covered in sweat. Blood runs from his nose down his chin. It seems that he came and cried in his sleep. He puts his underwear in a plastic freezer bag and throws it in the trash on his way to class.

His father is dead. What to do with his mother? There's nothing stopping him from having his way with her, but Lidija wouldn't want to. Ivor is slowly losing his patience. Soon he'll get his master's degree and leave home. A mother who can't orally satisfy her son is not a good mother. A mother like that, he doesn't need.

He takes a short holiday with his classmates. The entire literature department goes. He sits in the train compartment with five girls. They all want him, but he's not interested in a single one. Their mouths are too small.

The train creeps along. Ivor sees the creature from his dreams emerging from the forest, slowly, on the other side of the tracks. Instead of her mouth, his gaze falls on her body. As if pushing a fist into her, Ivor feels every inch of her sex: clitoris, labia majora, labia minora, vulva, vagina, cervix, uterus. He'd come from such a place once, but not by train. He regards the beast with great longing. She recedes into the trees, disappearing into their shade. He hides his erection from his colleagues with a volume of Byron.

WHEN HE RETURNS home from the trip, Ivor is determined.

"Tell me about my father!" he orders his mother.

Lidija stubbornly refuses. He grabs her by the face, roughly. He repeats, "Tell me about my father!"

Lidija falls silent, terrified. He throws her on the couch. He longs to rape her, he feels it. She becomes distraught when he starts unbuckling his belt.

"All right!" she says.

Ivor falls to his knees. "Start from the beginning."

"Your beginning was our end," Lidija says. "Everything went wrong."

His mother is crying. Her tears are making him hard. Maybe he wouldn't need to write a novel to hurt her.

"You're not my son."

Ivor thinks his mother is getting revenge. She's renouncing him.

"No, you don't understand. You're not my child. I didn't give birth to you."

"What?" Ivor says.

His nose begins to bleed again. He stuffs it with pieces of tissue.

"I can't have children," says his mother.

"And my father?"

"He wasn't your father."

His mother has shunned him. Artemidorus was right.

Sobbing, Lydia tells Ivor about the occasion of his birth. After her fifth miscarriage, her husband began to drink. He drank constantly. He lost his job. He drank even more. He tried quitting briefly. When the DTs struck, an ambulance had to come for him. He went crazy, telling Lidija he was seeing the Devil. He pounded his fist on the door. Screamed. Later, when he was finally hospitalized, the medics brought her papers she needed to sign. They told her that, during his ride in the ambulance, her husband had spoken of seeing children, of children waving at him. They were coming to the street to greet him. It was nighttime and one of the medics had looked out the foggy window of the ambulance. There was no one on the street. They were passing by the city cemetery.

"He was in recovery for a while, but I didn't go to visit him. He was hallucinating."

Ivor is silent. He is wearing his mother's bra under his shirt. Sweating.

"After two weeks, they released him from the

hospital. He walked home. When I opened the door, he was standing there with you in his arms."

"This is our son, Ivor," he said.

"We don't have a son," I said. "Whose child is this?"

"Ours."

"Who did you take the child from?"

"I didn't take him. I got him. There were other children, but Ivor is ours. He waved at me the longest."

The Abduction

God has given us hands, so we must work.

THREE TIMES THEY tried to pleasure me. It didn't
work. It was difficult to explain to them what pleasure even meant to us. I tried to describe my own
body with my hands, but of course I failed. They
peered at my palms. It wasn't possible to capture a
woman's physiognomy with gestures, but it seemed
they didn't understand hands either. What were
they for? Why were they there?

I won't even get into the lengths I had to go to
for a residency on the space station *Bitter Sun*, how
many people I had to call and how many times I had
to explain that the Writers' Society hadn't for years
sent me anywhere but the Alps and Mars, where I'd
already been hundreds of times. We all wrote the
same way: endless books that we packed with new
characters and advertisements. But I kept repeating myself because I'd been living in the same place

and thus lacked any inspiration. My characters all resembled one another, they just had different names, and of course the Society had argued that it wasn't worth sending me anywhere else when I showed so little talent on Earth. Unfortunately, my sexuality also developed around that rejection, mostly in solitude atop the Alps and on Mars, overwhelmed by commercial buzzwords and meaningless brands.

Sometimes private clients hired us to write ads on the black market and insert them "inconspicuously" into our interminable stories so they could avoid paying a commission to the Writers' Society. There was one writer, regularly cited as a role model, who in his day had written two identical books about the same spice—something that no longer existed, vegeta or fegeta if I'm not mistaken— and merely changed the title.

"Exactly the same books!" a woman from the Society cried. "What a genius!"

Fegeta was gone, I reckoned, but its ad campaign had survived. Of course, I didn't say anything, because I really wanted to go to *Bitter Sun*, and those who protested and advocated for the union rights of writers weren't sent there. Sure, we had our own association, but that association was your typical front for law enforcement agencies to monitor those engaging in freelance work and stashing their earnings in fake accounts. I spent most of my black-market money on new teeth and visits to the brothel. I didn't want anyone to know.

At one point, I'm not sure why, my short story's theme shifted to the Black Death and the heightened sex drive of plague victims. The Society immediately cautioned me, because it was impossible to incorporate proper ads into inappropriate content. But I couldn't stop writing elaborate scenes in which people were fucking incessantly, infected with a pathological desire to live forever—even, if necessary, by rape. I knew a lot about pathological longing, but I couldn't address it openly; companies didn't advertise through my books as it was, and insisting on such deviance would've destroyed my reputation completely. So I drafted and deleted sex scenes, drafted and deleted, until at one point I could no longer draw a distinction between what was inappropriate and what was an integral part of my craft. The texts we mass-produced were unreadable trash. In my lack of talent I didn't differ all that much from other writers, but I made less money.

I don't know, then, what miracle landed me on *Bitter Sun*, given that my writing hadn't improved at all. I think someone at the brothel had put in a good word, maybe some fellow writer who was also stuck censoring himself in order to work. I packed at the speed of light and let myself feel happy. I waited for congratulations from the Writers' Society, but there was nothing.

WHEN THEY TRIED to pleasure me the first time, I didn't immediately grasp what they wanted because they were touching my back. They ran something metal down my spine. They tapped on each vertebra as if looking for an opening. At first I thought they were massaging me, then attempting to access my spinal cord, but it dawned on me that they might be looking for something that had nothing to do with my back. It seemed like they were tapping me with a thermos—the object reminded me of one. They were saying something, but I couldn't understand, and I gathered that they couldn't understand me either. Had they asked me what I was, what I did for a living, I would've said without thinking that I was an economist, or a marketing specialist—but we didn't get to that. They spoke as if they were seducing me, that much I understood, and they certainly weren't discussing my profession; they just threw me on my stomach and busied themselves with my back, my crooked spine.

Finally! I thought. *Finally someone's touching me without gloves.*

They placed me in a pavilion with a bed, an armchair on one side, and a modular synthesizer on the other. They'd hung a framed photograph of Earth on the wall. The frame was lovely, lovelier than the small photo at least. I didn't pay much attention to the synthesizer because I was completely unmusical. I noticed, however, that there weren't any speakers, which confused me. I could fiddle with the buttons and dials with no consequences for others' ears or my own. Soon they brought in an old, broken keyboard and a sleeping bag with a long zipper, and I realized that sound didn't interest them at all. They wanted to observe the work of the fingers. They wanted to see how I used my hands, what I did with them.

The pavilion was disproportionately large in relation to the items they'd put inside, especially the photo of Earth. But perhaps that lack of proportion was a flaw only to my eyes, while to them it was the definition of harmony and good taste. A big Earth in a small frame, me in an oversize bed, a bed in an oversize room, and an oversize room in a tiny universe. Maybe they saw and understood things and relationships better than I did. Their ads were certainly of higher quality than ours, but that wasn't saying much.

Bitter Sun had a regular clientele who would vacation there for its beautiful artificial beaches, and reserved only a small space for writers, a room where the wealthier entrepreneurs wouldn't be caught dead. Still, I was thrilled to be there: I could go to the beach whenever I wanted and write marketing copy while lying on the sand that was never too hot—the Sun had been cooling for years, burning less intensely than before. In the first few days I wrote two ads: the first was for a diuretic syrup and the second for underwear that never needed to be washed. They were for the same well-known manufacturer, and I received a generous fee. I had about twenty other ads on my schedule that I needed to weave into a story which had two narrative branches: the first was about the Black Death and a woman who flees to the mountains to escape a wrecked plague survivor who wants to rape her because he heard it could restore his former looks; and the second was about a young girl whose parents lose her on Mercury, and her experience growing up in isolation. Within the story I was supposed to mention several types of cheese, a banana-rose hybrid, cologne, mushy food for astronauts, and a bunch of equally trivial things I'd never tried. It often happened that I'd write something in error about a certain product and the clients would contact me through the Society, requesting that I correct it in an upcoming chapter. The stories forked, meandered, and led nowhere, so I didn't have to pay attention to the congruence of time or the cohesion of the plot. Anything worked. I wrote as if on the diuretic I'd advertised in the story, but no one objected. Least of all the clients.

WHEN THEY TRIED to pleasure me the second time, I laughed. I was seized by a fit of hysterical laughter, in fact, because they tickled the soles of my feet with the same object from before, and then used it on my armpits. I couldn't remember ever having laughed so hard. Their silhouettes hovered over me, and they laughed too.

"Laughter. Well, we do have something in common after all," I said.

"Yes, we do," a voice replied.

Astonished, I beheld them as if for the first time: the creatures looked like me, they had a face and a smile. Where arms would be, there was nothing, but they had legs, a torso—somehow I hadn't noticed this before. What had previously seemed like an insurmountable difference suddenly became a nuance. But why, then, couldn't they find the place they were looking for? I was in no hurry to explain its location to them. I was enjoying their commitment to my body, the intimacy that was developing between us.

The gloves for rent at the brothel had spikes on the fingertips, and every time one of the prostitutes touched me, I felt like I was leaving my own body and entering one of the stories I was writing. The prickling would usually begin at the nape of my neck, where our species was most sensitive, and then continue along the temples and behind the knees. Within seconds I'd be coming and swearing obscenely. Then I would erupt with rage over not being able to hold out longer, and not being able to reciprocate their touch because the pleasure had rendered my hands completely numb. I ground my teeth so much during each session that it was no wonder I had to buy a new set every other week.

THE THIRD TIME they'd almost hit the spot, but then they went farther south. They touched my groin, which I certainly liked, but it clearly wasn't producing the desired effect. There was no sting in their touch, which prevented me from fully enjoying the game. At the same time, I was pleased that they were trying desperately to interpret the grimaces I was making. My gaze would occasionally slip to the image of Earth, and my thoughts would wander to the ads I still had to write. Sometimes I would plot out a violent scene, whose inclusion was inevitable if I wanted to mention the hybrid banana product that would earn me enough money to afford new teeth and as many as three trips to the brothel.

They were grumbling. The fact that my body was not functioning at all as they'd expected confused them.

"They've atrophied," I heard one of them say.

"Shame," someone else said.

I understood them, but I didn't understand them. I knew that our species was degenerating, but I didn't know why. And into what, exactly?

Shortly after their third experiment, I fell asleep and dreamed of spiked gloves, the tiny needles detaching and sticking me between my legs, where they had previously touched me without pain. I ground my teeth until I woke up abruptly. They'd taken the modular synthesizer out of the pavilion and replaced it with a TV showing the most grotesque thing I'd ever seen. I was shocked and repulsed, though I couldn't explain why. The way in which the man and woman were embracing was unnatural; they clung to each other, panting. Their noses were glued together, and their mouths, and the parts between their legs connected and separated with a squelch. The two bodies seemed like palms vigorously and spasmodically applauding the greatest abomination ever recorded. I was numb with disgust, but I didn't know how to turn off the TV, which was set at its highest volume.

"Can you turn this off?" I shouted, hoping one of them would hear me.

And indeed, a tall person (I say "person" because it actually was one) came and muted the TV, but the picture kept going. They looked at me and sat down next to me on the bed. We didn't talk, I just nervously squeezed my own fingers, intertwined them, folded my palms. They looked at my hands. Then I, too, looked down and saw that I was imitating the actions from the TV with my hands, and I brought them to my knees in horror. I wanted both of my fists to fall off in agony, to never make those gestures again. I observed the stranger and concluded that it was human. It had to be, we were too similar. I could count the differences on one hand. They operated objects and performed actions like we did, but they didn't need hands for it, or if they did, I couldn't see them. The person next to me had something between his legs, there was no doubt about it, but I still preferred to look at his nape, his temples, and imagine how this man would react if I touched him behind his knees, or ran my fingers along his neck.

BITTER SUN SLOWLY rotated and revolved around the Sun. I had a month to integrate all the products, tailor my plot to them, insert them into the story, and sell as many as possible with my inelegant sentences. My thoughts began and ended with personal hygiene aids, restaurant chains, and different types of nuts and dates. I didn't have time to consider myself or the way I was living or enjoy anything because the products I advertised took precedence. Hunched over, I waited for exhaustion and discouragement to overtake me, stress piling up like my sentences, displeasure grafting each one to the next, so that finally, incapacitated, I fell asleep on the beach, drooling in the sand. I think they found me like that and took me away. The space station's security system was always activated, so it wasn't clear to me how they got in, but they managed to take my sleeping body away without alerting any of the guards. When I woke up, all I saw was the pavilion and those faces that rolled me over onto my stomach. It was warmer than the beach, maybe due to the heat emanating from me.

The TV was on all the time, but I was no longer bothered by the scenes it played. Remarkably, they called those actions "fucking," but to me they were unrecognizable. We used the same words for completely different things.

I was thinking, of course, about all the money the clients would lose because I wouldn't be able to write ads for them, and I feared having to pay it back from my own pocket. I had two fake accounts where I deposited my earnings. In one, I kept money for the dentists and prostitutes, and in the other, I'd been saving up for my own pair of spiked gloves. I'd determined it would be an excellent investment, since I wouldn't have to go to the brothel as often and could easily masturbate at home.

The pain driving our orgasms was always the same: brief and paralyzing. We'd lose control of our own bodies, especially our hands, which otherwise never rested. I wrote nonstop; every thought had to be commodified, every piece of food typed out. Sleep rested the head, but not the hands, as there were some things we could do at night, without consciousness. Special computer programs had been written to prolong the work of our hands. During sleep our other motor skills would shut down to prevent sleepwalking, but our hands would continue their nocturnal life without us. They didn't really belong to us anymore.

WHEN I THOUGHT of people, I thought of advertising: what I could sell, and to whom, and how I could sell a person through an ad. Humankind had always been a bit foreign to me because I had no other needs aside from resting my hands. Nothing else interested me, not even buying or selling, but if your life was not material for good advertising, then it wasn't worth shit. So I hid my outings to the brothel, my obsession with idleness. But now I've deviated from the main story. Essentially, that man sitting next to me remained silent until I asked when I could return to *Bitter Sun*.

"Why do you want to go back?" he asked.

"I have to work," I said.

"Why?"

"I took an advance. I have to write about bananas."

The man laughed.

"What's wrong with bananas?" I asked, confused.

"It doesn't matter," said the man.

Had he had hands, he would've waved my question away, but he just shook his head.

"Do you know why we don't have hands?" he asked.

"No, why?"

He didn't reply right away.

"Hands are sometimes a serious problem," he said. "They tether a person to work."

Never before had I thought of hands this way. That is, I hadn't considered that without hands, I might be free. I lowered my gaze to my fingers again. I'd always regarded hands as indispensable, but even without them, there would be ways to do things with our mouths, noses, other parts of our bodies. The Writers' Society would find a way to make money. It would find a way to make us write about bananas, nuts and dates, elastic bands, and diuretics. About everything but ourselves, everything but unmarketable subjects.

"What is your profession?" the man asked.

I thought the word *marketing* would automatically shoot from my mouth like a cannon, but I had trouble getting it out.

"I don't know," I said. "I write ads, but it doesn't interest me."

"And what interests you?"

"Why am I here? Who are you all?"

He didn't want to answer me.

"What's your name? Can I at least know that?" I asked.

"My name is Sharmila."

"What is your profession?" I repeated his question.

"I work in neurodesign, computer manipulation of the body, especially neurons—but I'm most interested in humanoid robots."

"Sounds very interesting," I said. "But on our planet there aren't any more robots."

Sharmila laughed. Quite loudly.

"Why is that funny?"

Sharmila rested his head on my shoulder. I didn't know what to say. I was embarrassed because we never did such things. It was obvious that our customs were quite different.

"Are you uncomfortable?" Sharmila asked.

"A little, but it's okay," I said. "When can I go back to *Bitter Sun*?"

"I think the resort will be closing soon."

"I don't understand," I said. "It's the most popular destination. Very profitable."

I repeated "I don't understand" a few more times, at a loss to say anything else.

Bitter Sun was lying on its axis like Uranus, spinning strangely in space. Each rotation didn't take long, but we felt nothing of its speed. Though sometimes I wanted to be tormented by both gravity and rotation, to feel the movement of celestial bodies and the passage of time. It seemed that in life it was the sensory experiences that had the greatest weight, the greatest effect on us. If, for example, I were to stand by a moving train, I would feel something. When I stood next to people, I felt nothing. It was as if people had no weight—nothing to move, attract, or repel. They just were. Thinking about this tired me, but I couldn't help myself. At moments when I could no longer escape my own thoughts, I would withdraw money, head to the brothel, and indulge in some teeth-grinding. That was more pleasant for me, but now I couldn't do it.

"Everything will be all right," said Sharmila.

He bit the nape of my neck and that was the end of our conversation. My hands were paralyzed.

"Isn't 'Sharmila' a woman's name?" I asked him later.

"It's all the same to us," he said.

I was seized by a dizziness I'd never felt before.

"I wasn't completely honest," said Sharmila.

I looked at him wearily. I wanted to go back to *Bitter Sun*, and at the same time I never wanted to go anywhere else again. I liked spending my days in idleness, lounging in bed until noon, thinking about literature—but no more than before. Bananas, for example, weren't typically in the back of my mind. I didn't give a fuck about anything. It surprised me that I could pronounce so loudly and easily the very curses that had previously stuck in my throat: it wasn't appropriate to swear, but no one here reprimanded me for it.

"About what?" I asked.

"The nature of our relationship," he said. "I kept quiet about important matters."

"I know."

I wasn't sure if I wanted to know what Sharmila obviously wanted to tell me.

"Maybe it's better if I don't know," I added.

"Maybe," said Sharmila. "But still, things on Earth need to change."

I WASN'T SURE why there wasn't a fourth attempt. Perhaps in the meantime they'd caught on to everything and thrown their hands up, so to speak.

Due to weak sunlight, some of our vegetable crops were no longer thriving. Quite a few had perished because artificial heat was insufficient.

Photosynthesis had vanished from the face of the Earth, as had sex the way it once was, if I understood Sharmila. He stopped by every day to talk and said he was preparing me to return, but he never once mentioned *Bitter Sun*.

"Return where?" I asked him.

"Home," he said.

Besides Sharmila, I spoke to a dozen other people, but I didn't have the same relationship with them. They were more restrained: they never bit me, nor did they put their heads on my shoulder. They kept their distance, which would've suited me otherwise, but I'd changed and now their behavior was starting to bother me. I wanted to be close to everyone, not just one man.

"The others don't like me," I told Sharmila.

"Does that bother you?" he asked.

"Sometimes."

"That's a good sign."

Sharmila occasionally tried to talk to me about writing, but I made a point of avoiding the subject. What would I tell him, anyway? That literature disgusted me?

As if he were reading my mind, Sharmila said, "If you hate writing, what do you like?"

I didn't want to bring up the brothel.

"Freedom," I said, and then fell silent.

"I have a great idea for a story," Sharmila said. "Want to hear it?"

"Sure, but if the idea is really good, would you mind if I used it?"

"Of course not! So basically, before the Sun cooled, there was an institute for humanoid robotics on Earth. They called it 'Bitter Sun.'"

"I didn't know that," I said.

"Robots have never been humanoid enough for people," continued Sharmila, gazing into the distance as he spoke. "They always lacked something: gestures, phrasal verbs, nonchalance. There was, however, a group of scientists who weren't biased against artificial intelligence. As if intelligence is ever artificial!"

Sharmila paused. He rested his head on my shoulder with, it seemed, a great deal of tenderness. I thought of love, but the thought was short-lived, for he continued his story. He was almost whispering in my ear.

"Over time, this aversion turned into a serious intolerance. Demagogues began to denounce not only artificial intelligence, but intelligence in general: what we needed was human labor. Which, of course, is crazy, because people had stopped thinking about work; everything was done for them by robots."

He stared into my eyes, wanting me to say something, but I couldn't.

"In the meantime, some fanatics set fire to *Bitter Sun*, so the scientists had to move their operations elsewhere."

"Are you talking about a space station?" I asked.

"Yes, I mean the resort."

"And they continued to work there undisturbed?"

"I wouldn't say their work was undisturbed. It wasn't easy."

It sounded like he was speaking from his own experience, but all this had happened ages ago—Sharmila would've been long dead.

"There are no more robots on Earth," I said.

"Are you sure?" Sharmila asked.

My middle-of-the-night automated handiwork—I'd never thought of it as robotics. If intelligence was never artificial, as Sharmila contended, then how could that be work? Was I a robot?

"A call center was set up in Brussels, instead of the institute. A mockery of the building."

I knew exactly which building he meant. It truly was abhorrent.

"Are you tired?" he asked me suddenly.

"A little," I admitted.

"I should go," Sharmila said, but he didn't get up.

"Stay. The bed is big enough for both of us. I want to hear the rest of the story."

He obliged me.

"If you were writing ads," I told him as we reclined in bed, "you would be the highest-paid writer."

"I'm not so sure about that. We never lie."

SHARMILA WAS ALREADY awake when I woke up. He lay on his side, facing me. *Work makes the person* was written on the building of the nameless call center. I'd remembered that in a dream. Such a stupid, insulting claim!

"How often do you visit brothels?" he asked me.

"It doesn't matter."

"I'm interested."

"Often," I said.

"You have nothing to be ashamed of."

I knew that, but I was ashamed of my desires nonetheless. I sat up and moved to the edge of the bed. Sharmila's sudden bite hurt me, and I instantly came. My palms and elbows ached; my whole body was an open wound. I ground my teeth so much that a few cracked. I spat the pieces out on the floor.

"I'm glad you're not extinct," he said.

I had not yet regained control of my hands, but Sharmila bit me again. I cursed all the planets I could think of.

"You wanted us to emulate you, but look now. You have no control over your own movements. Half body, half computer program. You're less human than we are."

Sharmila seemed to be talking to himself. He bit me so many times I stopped counting. I no longer had a body. I had no hands for an hour; an unusable void stood in their place. Around me spread an invisible sphere of pleasure that took away all power of speech. I'd never felt better.

"The differences between us are shrinking. In a few months, they'll be completely gone."

"What differences?" I asked when I finally caught my breath.

"Look," Sharmila said.

I lowered my gaze to his groin. I thought of a banana. It reminded me of one. Sharmila didn't have hands, but this was a limb, too, he said. I remembered the footage they'd played for me when I'd first arrived. I finally understood those movements and that thing the couple was repeating: *That's it, baby! Yes!*

"My hands are programmed for work, not love," I said.

"Relax," Sharmila said. "You don't need hands."

I put my lips to his limb. Sharmila continued to bite the back of my neck. We both came quickly, though I couldn't determine if he'd lost the use of any parts of his body.

"Why did you abduct me?" I asked when I was able to speak again.

"The prostitutes," he said.

I'd gone to them constantly. I hadn't known they were informants.

"Are they robots too?"

"No, but they understand hard work better than anyone."

"They earn more than I do," I said, a little offended. "And I know what hard work is."

"Of course," Sharmila said in an appeasing tone. "That's why you're here."

He explained to me that he and his colleagues

wanted to return to Earth. They needed someone to reintroduce them into the human imagination.

"You want me to advertise you?" I asked.

"Yes. We'll pay you generously."

"More than a prostitute?" I asked.

Of course I, too, sold myself, but Sharmila was kind enough not to acknowledge it out loud.

"Do you agree?" he asked. His voice trembled, as if he were afraid of my answer.

"Yes," I said.

I'd never written about robots.

"Are you dying from a plague too?" I asked him.

"Only from human hands and filthy language," he replied.

He bit me again, but this time on the lip. I pushed my tongue into his mouth. Our noses touched. Sharmila lay on his back. I climbed on top of him. I learned from a robot. I imitated him in order to be human.

Δάφνη, or Daphne

I NEVER HAD any trouble recognizing Apollo's personal ads in *Start* and *Erotica*, old magazines from the eighties that I enjoyed leafing through whenever I was bored at home. I would lie in bed and read the "Lonely Hearts" section, sometimes aloud. I laughed at people's desperation, but I laughed at Apollo the hardest. Centuries had passed. Ours had been a bitter parting, but he still reached out regularly and waited patiently for me to forgive him.

"Beware," this ad read, "you may be ugly and misunderstood, you may have nothing, but it doesn't matter as long as you're rich in character, young, and emotionally resilient, code VIS VITALIS 234." Apollo sent messages into the past, bypassing time to get to me. He didn't care about the internet at all, though I'm sure he secretly followed all my social media profiles, maybe even my finsta. He always addressed me as a man in those funny messages. For Apollo I was the embodiment of masculinity, because he attributed all positive values to the male gender, while the things he most despised, and I loved, he considered feminine weakness. He stubbornly objected to the whole female gender. Not because he hated women, but rather because he blindly worshipped men.

I read his message several times. 3/13/1982. *Start* issue 343, list price thirty dinars. The magazine contained an interview with Orson Welles and an article about Ljubljana's resistance to the opening of a mosque. There was also a big feature about the Croatian island of Lastovo. "Will the booming tourist industry drown Lastovo?" wondered the journalist. I wished I could write to the Yugoslavs of the past, but I could only correspond that way with Apollo. I never replied to him though. I just laughed and that was usually the end of it. This time, however, I was attracted by the number 234. He was referring to a bus route. He wanted to see me. And I finally wanted to see him too.

The Greeks told a lot of lies about me and Apollo back in the day. After killing the huge snake that wanted to rape his mother beneath Mount Parnassus, filling in the hole in the ground and building a shrine to himself there, Apollo began to mock Eros. The Ancient Greeks remembered that part correctly, but then they made a mess of things. It turned out that Eros was a really shoddy marksman because he didn't actually shoot me or Apollo. His arrows landed in the bushes behind us, even though he'd aimed at us as we lay still under the laurel tree, whose leaves we'd been chewing during an earlier romp. I sank into a slight trance, but this was to be expected since no one penetrated by the god of male beauty could remain lucid. Our love ended tragically then, but I was hardly some frightened virgin who fled from Apollo and begged her parents to turn her into a plant. Politics doomed us. The Greeks could not write about it because women were forbidden to engage in politics, even when they were irresistible water nymphs like me.

Actually, I was a handsome boy, and that's why Apollo loved me so much: young men brought him their hair—snipped curls and long, wavy locks—which he cherished. So even though I was considered the most beautiful water nymph, I was a young man who'd offered his curls to god. My deed was declared a terrible offense. Apollo protected young men; I should've bestowed my virgin penance onto his sister, Artemis, but I was not in love with her. Apollo accepted my lock of hair and immediately wove it into his arrow.

"I will unleash the next plague in your name," he promised.

Short-haired, I fell into his arms. We made love under the watchful eye of his frowning sister.

"Let her be," he said. "Artemis just watches, she desires nothing more."

137

Apollo was both brilliant and revolting. Every time he climaxed you could hear the squawking of crows. They were the voice of his pleasure: hoarse and discordant. He was a god of dance and music, but his tongue tangled messily with mine as if I were deeply kissing him in river rapids and he couldn't catch his breath. Sometimes I'd lick his arrows and my tongue would bleed. That's why the Delphic priestesses called me "bloody." The epithet stuck. Later, historians would also describe me this way in their books.

The longer we were together, the louder Apollo's crowing grew, but the intensity of my pleasure slowly waned. My sisters assured me that men were, fundamentally, bad for me.

"They're all the same!" they said, unanimous.

"Perhaps," I said, but I wasn't convinced.

Apollo was his father's son: brutal and gentle at the same time, a softie fortified by faith in masculine strength and glory. He ridiculed women as the weaker sex, but his genitals transformed at night and he loved cunnilingus more than anything. I lapped him up like a shellfish. He was insatiable. My greatest boyish joy was to stick my head between his legs. I never knew if I would be greeted with semen or a clear wetness I could bathe in. He knew I loved water and he often pampered me. He was not a selfish lover. This redeemed him.

Others feared Apollo's arrows, but I was turned on by his cruelty. As a woman, I shared his acuity—I understood it. When he acted like a benevolent god, he became repugnant and foreign to me. The Greeks would later speak of metamorphoses, but never the most beautiful transformation: a feminine Apollo, gripping me with his thighs and crying when he came. Why didn't they write about that? They were afraid of male weeping. I wept too, of course, but out of helplessness. I fucked him roughly, but history remembered me as a delicate laurel branch dedicated to men's poetic inspiration.

I REMEMBER VIVIDLY my first prophetic dream. I often met Apollo at Delphi. He secretly introduced me to the hallowed and forbidden adytum, deep inside the temple. Usually I would put some fresh laurel in my mouth and chew it until my jaw ached. But that day I abstained. I felt nauseated all day, as if bile were pooling in my chest. Digestion tormented me. Apollo tormented me. At times I thought I might be pregnant, but that was just your typical girlish anxiety. God had initiated me in love, but he couldn't tell me anything about motherhood. Which was making me vomit too. While I was fighting this feeling of persistent nausea, Apollo became fixated on my armpits—he couldn't stop sniffing and licking them. I let him play with my body, but at one point I sank into the deepest sleep, feverish. Death was close, and my greatest joys—springs, river rapids, deep lakes—roiled with blood. God burst out of that water, grabbed me by the throat, and strangled me. The prophetic hallucinations of Apollo's priestesses were common, but the Pythian priestesses could never see very far into the future. Their eyes could only glimpse the outline of a tragedy. I could feel it as keenly as Apollo's tongue on my skin: I saw Europe changing, Greece collapsing—but for some reason Yugoslavia struck me the most. I gargled blood and swore. My lips cracked, I felt a chafing at the corners of my mouth, as if history were a huge phallus ramming itself down my throat, trying to tear me apart.

Apollo shook me for a few moments, begging me to forget the visions I'd seen. A beautiful woman must not speak of ugly things. He kissed my neck. He cried. He knew he'd lost me: no one who sees the future clearly can believe in god.

"Come back!" Apollo shouted. "Come back!"

Followed by: "Please, I love you," or something like that, but all I could sense was his fear. Now I sniffed at his body. History unraveled in my head like a ball of yarn, poisoning me. I vomited throughout the night. It was only at dawn that I briefly regained consciousness. Apollo embraced me.

"You can't come here anymore," he said. "It's too dangerous."

"Why?" I asked.

"The future is not for women," he said.

I vomited on him. Pythia came to our aid and put a hand on my forehead. Her power was an illusion because it came directly from Apollo, but I accepted the consolation. My whole body was on fire, as if he'd thrown me onto his hearth, by the tripod on which the Pythians sat and spoke with Apollo's voice in the future tense.

"Everything will be all right," said the priestess, but the voice was Apollo's and I didn't believe him.

God addressed me from both bodies. I wanted to talk to him about the Carolingians, the Berlin Wall, Yanis Varoufakis, but he kept telling me to forget everything, that all would be well. Years later, I'd find comfort in the fact that Apollo loved me so passionately he couldn't help imparting to me the visions he gave so sparingly to others. The future was rushing in; I frequently dreamed of it. There was no more room for Apollo in my mind. The nightmare of history pushed him out.

When he found me the next time in the adytum kneeling mournfully over a hole in the ground, crying and inhaling the ethylene that regularly induced the Pythians' hallucinations, Apollo pulled me up by the hair. I could clearly see the seventeenth century: I knew the sweet smell of ethylene would be discovered by the German Johann Becher. I knew that there would be a Germany, that there would be a Greece under Germany. I saw everything yet was powerless to do anything. Apollo dragged me by the hair, sweeping the floor with my body as he pulled me out of the temple. His tenderness was gone; he was furious. I could feel his erection.

When we arrived at the front steps, knowing that I despised him, he raped me.

Naturally I'd read the literature on Ancient Greek myths and rituals. Contemporary interpretations of Ancient Greece were their own ethylene hallucinations, but the humanists didn't always write nonsense. In the hole from which the temple of Apollo had sprung, the dismembered body of Dionysus was indeed rotting. When he'd caught me in the adytum, Apollo had instantly grasped that I was trying to summon the god of wine, and he'd become violently jealous. He couldn't stand my quest for intoxicating wine to free my tongue. The Pythians trembled in ecstasy while they prophesied in Apollo's voice, because the tripod they sat on was his lap. Apollo was enough for them. Occasionally I watched them climax from the sidelines. Their faces were distorted with pleasure. The priestesses couldn't see the horrors that had already happened in the future, and I envied them for that. In Apollo's embrace, time would stop; there was nothing but his engorged genitals and a wet bite on the neck. I needed a break, and Apollo couldn't help me. I needed strong Dionysian alcohol.

"Eros is a verb," wrote Anne Carson. She was right. Thinking about these verbs, about what would be left of the world after them, was reserved for the Pythians, for me. I wasn't sure men truly understood verbs, and the passage of time. They spent their lives in the jaws of conjugation. It had taken me centuries to finally accept that Apollo and I shared love, but not eros.

I was convinced that Eros was targeting neither him nor me that fateful day, but the ground on which we lay. As if he were targeting Greece and letting our history flow from his arrow. I clearly felt a change in my relationship with Apollo after that. Sometimes he hugged me frantically like I was dying, and other times he was calm and cheerful. He became elusive, like running water.

"We will never understand each other," said the lovestruck Apollo.

"*You'll* never understand *me*," I corrected him.

After my romance with Apollo, I became brutal. I witnessed events that I'd foreseen in the past—everything came true. I could influence some small things, soften the outcomes, but verbs devoured everything, and once the deed began, it was hard to stop it with sensible words.

In the early 1980s, for example, I worked briefly on a social and cultural magazine called *Woman* that explored the place and role of women and families. I wrote about women in socialist, self-governing Yugoslavia, which was enjoyable, but also depressing because I knew it wouldn't last: "According to the fascist perspective, women are incapable of working in the manufacturing sector. Women don't need schools or education." I knew, of course, that Apollo was reading me. I wondered, feigning naivete: "Who is to blame for the fact that women, for hundreds and hundreds of years, have been living in darkness and ignorance? That, for a long time, their course of action hasn't been clear?"

I BOARDED THE bus in the morning. I only tweeted a brief "I'm coming." Apollo had used the past to reach out to me, but I refused to go back. He'd contacted me through an erotic magazine, and I'd replied on a social network. I provoked him with the idea that the future was mine, that I belonged to it no matter how uncomfortable it was.

It was cold and my nipples were visible under my sweater. Knowing Apollo, he'd interpret it as a clear sign of desire. I braced myself for his cruel teasing. Would he be glad to see me? My prophetic visions did not reveal things that concerned me directly. I was hidden from myself. I found it impossible to imagine our conversation, to hear in advance the first words I would speak to Apollo's face after a century of silence.

I got out at the last stop, looked around, noticed a lone elm tree, and lightly stepped toward it. In a few years the tree would be gone; I regarded it with sadness, from a distance, as if it were a mirage. When I got close enough to the elm, I was stunned. I barely recognized him. Dionysus Zagreus shook the flask in his hands. He would occasionally bring it to his mouth, but he wouldn't take a drink.

Turning, he saw me and the flask fell out of his grip. Wine spilled ominously on the grass. The last time I'd seen Dionysus he'd been hidden in a hole, dismembered, but now he was standing in front of me, disguised as a handsome stranger, almost unrecognizable.

"Apollo is squatting in the hole now instead of you?" I asked.

"I wouldn't call that place a hole," Dionysus said.

"Fuck, before Freud came along that's what we used to call the unconscious."

We both laughed, despite feeling the effects of centuries of bitterness and exhaustion. Knowledge didn't set us free, but we both enjoyed it. Unlike Apollo, Dionysus wasn't bothered by my cursing. If anything, it seemed like my "fuck" delighted him. This didn't surprise me: what Apollo built, Dionysus allegedly demolished. Decency was the first thing to go.

"It's been a long time," Dionysus said.

"We haven't had a reason to hang out."

"Then why did you come?"

"I was bored," I lied.

He shrugged. He knew I was lying. He stared at the spilled blood. The ground was hard; it hadn't absorbed a drop.

"Why did you flee to the Balkans?" he asked. "You could've gone anywhere. Why here?"

"I don't know," I said. "It's close to Greece. Maybe that's why."

"I think you like the chaos that reigns here. As if the place was untouched by Apollo."

"Do you always talk about yourself in the third person?" I asked, tartly.

While we were together, Apollo had carefully hidden Dionysus from me. The Greeks knew that every god was plural. The gods took other forms—human, animal, other gods—but metamorphosis meant a complete change for the Hellenes. Nothing of Dionysus was in Apollo, even though they were the same person. Apollo was several things, but never at the same time. The Great Apollo never held a wineskin. Dionysus Zagreus never held a lyre.

I'd known nothing about psychoanalysis, of course, when I'd first fallen in love with Apollo. Family ties with Olympus had seemed simple in my youth, like drinking cold water from an underground spring, but eros had irrevocably changed my view of the world, of fathers, mothers, sisters. I wanted to see Apollo's other, secret side—the stranger buried in the adytum, the god he presented to naive people as his younger brother.

Even before I'd sensed what a dichotomy he was, I'd been drawn to the idea of Dionysian phallophoria. Often, disguised as a mortal Greek woman, I'd worn winged genitals in the Dionysian processions. I'd briefly considered joining the maenads, but there wasn't enough lust in their mania, and it turned me off. The idea of a dismembered man was appealing to me, but when they were initiated into madness, the maenads didn't think about blood-thirsty sex. Only revenge mattered to them. I didn't discuss this with Apollo, though I'm sure he sensed my desire and thus buried Dionysus even deeper when in my company.

"Euripides wrote the last meaningful thing about you. You were popular, but no one under-stands you anymore."

"I know," Dionysus said.

I wanted to start an argument. I was angry and couldn't calm my heart: it was pounding wildly. When Dionysus briefly lifted his gaze, I saw Apollo in him. He could've gone mad in various ways, but Dionysus just squeezed my fist lightly to encourage me. There wasn't a shred of vindictive anger in his touch. It was as if he'd drowned all of his negative emotions in wine.

"Do you have any more?" I asked.

He pulled a bottle from his pocket. I drank it down in one gulp. Blood rushed to my head, and I reddened. I could hold my liquor, but now I stag-gered as if I'd drunk a whole barrel of young wine. Dionysus took me by the upper arm so I wouldn't fall.

"I'm sorry," he said.

The force of those words brought tears to my eyes.

"You have too many names, too many faces," I said. "What should I call you? Zagreus, Dionysus,

Bacchus? Boisterous? Dionysus Androgynous? Mister Phallic? Dionysus the Rapist?"

"Rape is an Apollonian value. I prefer to liberate women."

Dionysus was still holding my arm. He wouldn't let go.

"You really think you're a liberator? How about Dionysus the Debauchee? Dionysus the Savior? I'll die laughing! Who invented all these stupid epithets? People are truly idiots."

"You've always been emotional," said Dionysus after I vomited on his shoes.

"What did you put in my wine? Poison?"

"Of course," he said.

"Of course," I repeated.

"Don't worry, you're not going to die. You'll just be a bit sick."

"I was sick as soon as I saw you!"

My tongue went numb. My mouth dried up, but my sight and my mind were not clouded. I watched Dionysus the Seducer with his long hair. I could clearly hear his voice ringing out:

"While the poison has you in its grip, I should explain what's going to happen."

I looked at him, frightened.

Only a fool, I thought, *only the worst fool would respond to an anonymous personal ad in* Start.

The poison was causing me to slowly lose the feeling in my legs.

"Nice of you not to wear a bra," he said, shoving his hand under my sweater.

148

"I knew it!" I shouted, but all Dionysus could hear was my gurgling.

"Relax," he said. "You'll choke on your own saliva."

He gently spread my lips apart with his fingers and poured more wine into my mouth. My heart was pounding harder. He held up my head. I concentrated on the label of the bottle Dionysus had gotten me drunk with: T'ga za jug. Served me right for drinking such swill.

"A transgression is a transgression, and you must be punished. The breakup of Yugoslavia has hurt you, but not enough."

I imagined the worst: he would rape me and turn me into a grapevine. What else would a drunken god do? But then out of the tree emerged Apollo's twin sister, Artemis Laphria, the goddess of hunting and political rallies. The Spartans honored her by whipping their boys and letting them bleed on her altar. She was crueler than Apollo. The nymphs who were her companions were happy to recount the events they'd witnessed: she'd killed men, punished women—even her own offspring. If Apollo was disgusting, she was thrice as bad. It wasn't clear to any of the nymphs why I'd chosen a cruel brother over an even crueler sister: "If you love bloodthirst, you should worship Artemis."

Not only did I not love her, I despised her.

"That arrow Eros launched when you and Apollo were lying under the tree," Dionysus said. "The one that landed in the bushes . . ."

". . . struck me right in the heart," finished Artemis.

"You shouldn't have been crouching in the bushes and spying on your brother," Dionysus told her.

"I was curious."

I choked on wine and saliva. I couldn't take another drop. Artemis looked at me lovingly. My hatred deepened.

"Well, this is awkward," said Dionysus. "The lovely nymph believes in psychoanalysis and thinks I'm Apollo."

He laughed, but he was as sad as I was. He wasn't enjoying this play.

"On the other hand, the lovely nymph is not aware of your deception," he said. "How many times have you transformed into your brother?" he asked her. "Ten, twenty?"

Artemis shook her head.

"More? Fifty?"

Now Dionysus was confused.

"I lost count," said the goddess.

The thought of having made her come so many times filled me with despair. All of Apollo's tears of joy had actually been hers.

"Will you admit everything you did to hurt her?" Dionysus asked Artemis.

I glared at him. He was still holding up my head with his hand. I no longer had any feeling from the neck down. Artemis stood leaning against the tree, silent. She just gazed at me longingly. My humiliation was complete: the god of wine kept his other hand on my breast. He was the greatest tragedian, the dramatist of dramatists. The mask he wore was excellent. I couldn't penetrate it. He was there because there was no greater tragedy than mine: I knew what would happen to the Balkans, to the whole of Europe, to North America—but I didn't know what would happen to me. He must have enjoyed my suffering.

I closed my eyes. Why hadn't I known, why hadn't I felt the difference between Apollo and Artemis? In the most intimate moments, I should have known who I was giving myself to. Surely there'd been a difference. In their touch, kiss, chokehold, light slaps on the back. Whose arrows had I licked, whose bow had I drawn? I hadn't paid attention to the quiver: Had it been Apollo's gold one or Artemis's silver? Above all, I wanted to know which of them had raped me: Brother or sister? Which had pulled my hair and made me hate the Greek soil? The questions overwhelmed me, and as if he could feel my despair, Dionysus poured more cheap wine down my throat. He wiped the red trail at the edge of my lips with his sleeve and continued as if nothing had happened:

"The political rallies held before the collapse of Yugoslavia. Tell her who organized them."

"I don't want to."

"On June 28, 1989, your birthday," Dionysus told me, "Milošević gave a speech at Gazimestan."

"Stop it!" Artemis said.

"But you are the goddess of political rallies and imperialist ambitions, why aren't you proud of that? Wasn't the Kosovo Field a nice birthday present?"

Had I devoured a field of nightshade, I still would've been less sick. I was vomiting from what I was being forced to listen to.

"Artemis loves you so much that she was jealous of the country where you were living. She literally tore it to pieces."

"If you don't shut up, I'll shut you up myself!" Artemis screamed.

"Again?" Dionysus asked, his tone calm.

"Remember what lies the Greeks told to redeem your character the last time," he continued. "They put it all on Hera."

"Poor Hera!" said the goddess, full of spite.

Anger was distorting her face.

"You've been holding her in your arms long enough," she said. "Give her to me. I want her desperately!"

Artemis lunged toward us, her arms extended, but Dionysus hugged me tightly and took a few steps back.

"I'm not sure that's possible," he said.

The change was imperceptible. Like a breeze overturning a leaf, Dionysus changed his form: Apollo held me in his arms. That turning point reminded me of Euripides: When you expect it, it doesn't happen. When there is no hope, the gods find a way. That's how this plot concluded too.

But the three of us were far from the ending. Apollo and Artemis stood facing each other, as full of desire as I was of wine. It nearly poured from their ears and nostrils. They wanted me, and they wanted each other. Euripides's simple, wise words were no longer enough to conclude the tragedy: reality grew more complicated. We'd come a long way from the Ancient Greeks—a long way indeed, and we'd fallen even deeper. In those depths we found the unconscious: no family was beyond tragedy anymore. Dionysian wine no longer cured sorrow alone.

Artemis once more passed through the elm tree to be purified, but it's impossible to ritually purge desire from an aroused body. She was irrevocably tainted by it, a virgin rolling in the mud of longing. She would spend her days drifting through different cracks and openings, through different women, in an attempt to forget me, but still—she'd never succeed. There were plenty of nymphs, but none was the arrow that pierced her. Eros was the cruelest god.

As Apollo quickly carried me away on his swan, beyond the reach of the furious and amorous Artemis, I wondered if the sister and brother would eventually slaughter each other. After all, we were in the Balkans, so the question was a natural one. I could see the answer clearly, like a trace of sweat on Apollo's upper lip, but my tongue, numb from North Macedonian wine, wouldn't let me speak of the future. Dionysus was indeed the Liberator: he'd gotten me drunk, relieving me of my duty to prophesy. I closed my eyes. The Socialist Federal Republic of Yugoslavia no longer existed. I didn't care about the rest.

MCSB

For Brane

YOU STAND FROZEN in a field of corncockle.
Your armpits are damp with sweat. You got very
drunk last night. You're not really in a field of
corncockle, but it's as if you are: you think of the
toxins contained in these types of wild carnations,
you think of saponins and muscle spasms. You see
yourself chewing on a plant like a cow because you
think it's healthy, then dying. Dying in agony, but
no one will help you. That ugly thought suddenly
vanishes. As if someone has lifted a veil from your
eyes. You look out at the cultivated terrain and the
field-research forms you're holding in your hands.
How many minutes have you been standing still?
Five or more? Ten? Time encircles your legs—not
time, stalks of wheat. You kick them away. You're
stepping on someone's bread. You lose your mind
and you don't know why. Clouds are gathering

above you. It was clear until a little while ago. You even wrote on the form that there were no clouds, but now? You update the cloud cover to 60 percent. The whole document will be illegible: as soon as you write one thing, you have to change it. Nature contradicts your every word.

There are numerous sections to fill out. You had to enter your full name, the date (May 5), the locality (Mala Mlaka), the temperature (17 °C), the transect number (E4788 N2530), the coordinates (x: 457245 y: 155715), and a brief description of the habitat (a blend of shrubs, meadows, low and high crops). You paused at first when filling in your name; for a moment you couldn't remember it. Elis, your name is Elis. Your father gave you that name because he loves Trakl: *A golden boat, Elis / rocks your heart in the lonely sky*. You know the whole poem by heart; you've heard those verses from your father's mouth so many times that you've grown sick of them. You despise your name, but the birds the poet wrote about—those you could never hate. The gaze that others turn inward, you've turned to the sky. Every day you thank Trakl for that.

YESTERDAY YOU WERE at your sister's birthday party. You were nervous because every now and then your eyes wandered to your brother-in-law's hands, cutting the cake. He held the knife like a sword. They don't have children; that matters to you. You would feel worse if they did. You will never admit how much you love him.

"Do you want a piece?" he asked you.

You nodded, but you didn't mean the cake. His movements were much sweeter. You're in love. You don't dare tell anyone. You'll take the secret to your grave.

You take a sip of black tea from a thermos. The break is over, and you move on. You have to finish your survey by nine o'clock. Every hundred meters you stop, you take pictures in every direction with your phone (as proof that you went out into the field), and then for five minutes you calmly observe and listen to the landscape. The form has two concentric circles printed on it: a smaller one, representing thirty meters in diameter, and a larger one, representing one hundred meters in diameter. You are in their center, stuck like a scarecrow. But you're not here to scare off the birds. Your job is to count them and note their location in the circles: those that fly over, and those that perch in the field, on branches and stumps. You also have to document the species that can only be heard, not seen. The farther the birds are from you, the farther you are from yourself, but there's nowhere to write that. The form doesn't have space for private observations. The Croatian Ministry of Agriculture doesn't pay fifteen hundred kuna for the work of reflecting and remembering.

Your eyes move over the circles. On the first page

you recorded *Mot. fla.*, *Syl. atr.*, *Syl. com.*, *Stur. vul.* (eight specimens), *Cor. corax.*, *Cor. corni.* (in flight). After that—nothing. You're not satisfied. Too few birds. They're avoiding you. You hear a cuckoo in the distance. Again. You write it for the fifth time outside the circles, on the margin: *Cuc. can.* You put a bold question mark next to it. Did you really hear the bird or did you just imagine it? Again: *Cuculus canorus*. You try to spot it, but in front of you stretches only the lush field of wheat and barley. There's nothing in the sky, Elis, nothing. The empty circles tighten around you like an iron band. And you feel depleted. Just before, you were sitting on the cut grass, breathing deeply, but you don't feel at ease. The quieter the environment, the deeper your turmoil.

Nature doesn't rest, however. The sky diligently keeps gathering clouds, as if it wants to collect them all. According to your rough estimate, the cloud cover now exceeds 75 percent. The air temperature drops sharply. You can feel the difference on your skin. The wind, which was completely absent at first, now upends the papers in your hand with great force, threatening to blow them all over the field. You don't understand the sudden shift. Is this kind of weather common for early May? You don't know, you're not a meteorologist. You're not even a biologist, but rather a banker, a bird lover, an amateur ornithologist. You came to enjoy yourself, but how do you enjoy yourself with only your own company?

Five minutes become an eternity. You stand and wait, the hands on your watch not moving. You hear a cuckoo again, loud, like it's flying past your head. It sails over the property, but what's not clear is how that birdsong is managing to reach your pricked ears, given that the wind is blowing the opposite way. When the voice stops, you obediently head in the direction it came from. But it's a direction not shown on the map. You're moving away from your vantage point. Diverging from the path. You walk slowly. Your legs are not yours. To encourage yourself, you recite Trakl in your head: *How long, Elis, you have been dead. // Your body is a hyacinth, / The monk dips his waxen fingers into it.* Suddenly you understand: the voice that recites the verses in your head is not yours. You are forced to pronounce them. You keep walking. You're sweating. You come to the edge of a forest. One more step and you've entered it. You don't want to be, but you're inside. The cuckoo's there too. You can hear it. It's panting loudly like an aroused man. You're dead, Elis, dead. You ask yourself, without any sentimentality, who will dip their fingers into you when you die? Your father? Sister? Brother-in-law?

If you were walking up the stairs to your apartment, you'd count each step. You've always done that, but now such obsessive behavior doesn't make sense. There's no ascent here. Walking on a flat surface poses no challenge. If you were climbing the clouds to reach the sky, you would count them, Elis, just as you count money at the bank every day.

Millions, billions. Instead of kuna, verses have now accompanied you, frightened, into the forest. It's your father's fault, of course. What a stupid name he gave you. You sound like a victim, not a banker.

Iva, the young woman who used to hold the job of Monitor of Common Species of Birds (MCSB) here, abruptly withdrew from the project. She left Mala Mlaka and even the nearby Botinec neighborhood to you. She gave no explanation. You remember her once complaining that she'd met an intrusive villager in the field who'd wanted to introduce her to his only son. Their house was on the other side of the forest (her words lodged in your memory), hemmed in by trees and a field of grain. As you walk, you remember what Iva said: their whole yard was overgrown with weeds, and for every stalk of wheat there was a shoot of corncockle. Despite having died off elsewhere, the plant had thrived at the home of the father and son. You immediately want to see that corncockle. You want to see that bachelor she mentioned. Actually you don't want to see him. Where did that idea come from? You've clearly plotted the house's coordinates on the map so you can avoid it more easily. The desire to go there has come out of nowhere. It's imposed itself on you, just like the cuckoo's voice. Planted itself. You're confused. You're thinking about a man you've never seen. The cuckoo's voice follows you right to his door. *When the blackbird calls in the black wood, / Elis, this is your descent.*

You can't hear the blackbird. Only the beating of your own heart. Excitement, like the cloud cover, exceeds 90 percent.

SOMETIMES THOUGHTS HAVE a life of their own. Yours are roaming on unnavigable paths, jumping nimbly like chamois. They climb to places no one else can reach. Now that you've come out of the forest and seen the house Iva was talking about, there are millions of these chamois. You can't count them all: they multiply like the dirty pictures you've accumulated on your computer. Among those images is a family photo of your brother-in-law standing shirtless. He's hugging your sister with his right arm, and you with his left. That left arm is dearer to you. You would cut off the other one.

You knock on the door. An old man opens it.

"My son," he tells you as if you're already acquainted, "is sitting in his room. Go to him."

You resist his command.

"Who are you?" you ask. "What is this house?"

You know he won't answer. You stand there, rooted. The old man pushes and pulls you like you're a stubborn mule. Your feet slide on the linoleum.

You almost tell him, *I'm an influential man—I'm rich!* But the old man is not interested in your money. You can feel it. For him and his son, the body is the only currency. He keeps pushing you. He opens the door wide with his foot. You see the bed.

Your brother-in-law is sitting on it. He's no longer naked only to the waist. You know you're dreaming, but you don't care. You'd give all the money in the bank to make this come true. You extend your right hand, which embraced him in the family photo.

The creature rises from the bed and hugs you. You know, Elis, that it's not your sister's husband. You know it, but you can't help yourself. The creature slowly passes its palm over your eyes as if lulling you to sleep, but you're already asleep. You don't need to be persuaded. You didn't get lost. You're convinced you came of your own free will. Periodically the image of your brother-in-law flickers to the image of the creature: It is monstrous. It looks half bird, half man. Its beak is huge like a raven's. Its face is covered with gray feathers. Its chest is a man's. The stripes that line its thighs are a cuckoo's. Strong legs end with claws. Your father cursed you with your name, but nature was much crueler to this creature. His desire feeds off yours. You can't imagine a worse punishment.

You lie on the bed (which could more accurately be described as a "nest"). *The bells sound softly in Elis' breast / In the evening, / When his head sinks into the black cushion.* You are, of course, that Elis, but you don't know exactly what that black cushion is. You don't know if the creature is penetrating you or vomiting in your mouth. Something is happening to your body. The spasms won't stop. You're nauseous. Numb, as if you've eaten all the corncockle around the house. Your body is paralyzed. You don't control it anymore. You've had uncontrollable longings before, but this is much more terrifying. Your eyes are closed the entire time. When you open them, you stand frozen in the field. You're sweating. You look at the cultivated terrain and the field-research forms you're holding in your hands. How many minutes have you been standing still? Five or more? Ten? You need to call Iva immediately. You don't want the monitor job anymore. MCSB is not for you. You feel weak. A stabbing sensation within your abdomen. If you didn't know better, you'd say that what you feel under your skin is a large bird's egg.

Dorica Kastra

AT FIRST, there were four of us in the marriage: Otis Tarda, Runio Clacla, Dorica Kastra, and me. But since the Family Law stipulated that each marriage had to have an odd number of spouses, we started thinking about the kind of person we wanted to add to the family. Otis was against deviant and dominant people, but Runio and I wanted just such men. Dorica abstained, so Otis was outvoted.

"He'll be ours," I said.

Runio hugged and kissed me passionately. Otis left the room. He couldn't look at us, he was so angry. Dorica, whom we all preferred to call Kastra, rushed after him to offer comfort.

"That's why we need a fifth person so badly," Runio said. "Our marriage is falling apart."

He was right. Lately it had been getting harder and harder to keep us together. Kastra treated everyone equally: she kept us all at the same distance. Otis and I still got along well. Although his relationship with Runio was also passionate, they often quarreled. A fifth person would surely help. The Ministry had already sent us a warning to look for someone, or else we would have to pay a steep fine. None of us earned much money. That's why a fifth person was essential for us: they would share the financial burden. We needed someone who would cheer up Otis while at the same time helping Kastra relax and do a better job carrying her weight.

"All families have troubles," Kastra once told me, but it seemed to me that our situation was more dire.

We were curled up together and I stroked her hair. Her scalp was covered in scabs because she often picked at it out of nervousness. She'd been living with us a few months at that point, but she was still a stranger to me. I'd lain above her body a hundred times, I could find her in a crowd—but I didn't really know her. She stubbornly refused to undress completely. If Otis, Runio, and I had talked openly then, I'm sure we would've realized that each of us was holding a different woman in our arms at night.

"Is it my fault that Otis and Runio argue so much?" she asked.

"No," I lied.

OTIS, RUNIO, AND I had gotten along well before Runio had brought home Kastra in a fit of jealousy. He'd wanted change, so he'd ushered in chaos. Kastra was exceptionally delicate. The three of us were boors in comparison. But once you'd admitted someone into the family circle and reported it to the Ministry, what was done was done. Runio was regretful, but there was no going back. Kastra numbed us. For several months she nearly emptied Otis of his desire. He showed no libido anymore. Distraught, Runio tied him to the bed and whipped him bloody. I wasn't there to stop it because Kastra and I had gone on a short trip together, in order to get to know each other more intimately. But pleasure eluded us. At times it seemed Kastra was asexual, but she assured us that wasn't the case. We simply couldn't satisfy her. That's why she developed nervous tics. Our marriage became a heavy burden for all of us. Worst affected was Otis, who always gave himself fully, without hesitation, in love. The fact that Kastra didn't want him was killing him.

"I can't take it anymore," Otis told me a few weeks after Kastra had joined our family. "That woman doesn't know what she wants."

"She knows," I said. "Problem is, she doesn't want us."

"But then why did she go for Runio?"

"I don't know," I said. "I really don't know."

Runio tried to explain that Kastra flirted with him when he first met her, but Otis and I couldn't accept this because she'd never flirted with us. His descriptions of the seductive Dorica Kastra were incompatible with the woman we were now all forced to live with and support. To make matters worse, she brought nothing to the marriage: no desire, no excitement, no money. Each of us tried to win her over separately, then all together—we even tried role-playing—but nothing helped. Her personality slowly drained all our joy. She was a spoiled baby who sucked her thumb and contributed nothing. Instead of a wife, we had a child.

"The person I want," Runio confided in me, "should be androgynous and insatiable. That's all I care about."

"I want a beautiful woman," Otis said.

His anger had faded quickly. This was the first time in months that we'd sat at the table without Kastra.

"A beautiful androgynous woman with insatiable sexual appetites," I summarized.

"What do you want?" they asked me.

"You two."

They laughed in unison.

"I want someone who'll keep us in line," I said. "Someone intelligent."

"Naturally," Otis said. "We don't want someone to bore us in three days."

He sighed mournfully. I knew he was thinking of Kastra.

"She's not stupid," I said.

"I know. She just acts like it."

Runio hugged him from behind. Otis froze for a moment, then relaxed.

"I love you," Runio told him.

Just as I was about to suggest I join them in bed, I noticed that Kastra was standing in the doorway. She looked disheveled, wild. For a moment it seemed like she was looking at us with frustration and hatred, but then she smiled, and the impression quickly evaporated. My heart sank. I didn't know what to say. If she joined us, she would ruin everything. I decided to sacrifice myself.

"Kastra and I can go for a walk. You two go to bed."

She looked at me blankly. I wanted to pull her by the hair, but I had to keep my aggression to myself.

We didn't stay out for long. We just strolled around the shopping mall a couple of times. I bought her a small gift for our approaching anniversary. She thanked me and gave me a chaste peck on the cheek, which annoyed me. I knew that, had they been in her place, Otis and Runio would've kissed me differently. Not innocently and certainly not on the cheek.

Back at home, I sprawled on the couch and

propped my feet up on the table. Kastra immediately went to her room. From Otis's room came the sound of loud panting. I briefly closed my eyes, imagining his and Runio's every move. They were sweaty and, knowing Runio, Otis was probably bound by a leather belt. Their gestures were almost theatrical: the pleasure was staged. Surely they were filming themselves. If so, I'd ask to see later what they'd gotten into while I was gone. I wanted to oil up my hands and join the game, but Kastra had spoiled my mood so completely that all I could do was lie on the couch.

I tried to imagine a fifth member of our family. If it were up to Otis alone, we'd get a woman more submissive than me. I could practically feel her: long hair, long legs, a beauty who'd make easy money and let Otis do whatever he wanted, including those things he never dared ask of me. Otis Tarda was a strange creature, at once a great sadist—literally a devotee of the Marquis de Sade who wanted friends, not lovers—and a romantic introvert who looked for every opportunity to surrender to my and Runio's control. But Tarda was consistent in this contradiction, and we were happy to indulge him. He was two people, and that's how we addressed him: when he was rough, he was "Tarda," and when he sought our roughness, we purred, "our darling Otis." It was hard for me to imagine a person I could've wanted more.

If we had chosen our new member according to the Runio metric, we would've gotten someone genderqueer, which I would've happily obliged. Runio was far more flexible in his tastes than Otis or me. He preferred a chameleon, someone capable of being anything and everything. It seemed that the promise of a multifaceted person had initially attracted him to Kastra, but in the end the chemistry hadn't materialized. I knew his mistake bothered him, but I wouldn't let him torture himself over it. Perhaps we should've left the decision about the next partner to him, to show how much we still trusted him.

Runio knew, of course, that I loved Otis more. He could feel it. In a way, it was my fault that Runio had dragged a fraud into our household—or our ménage, as we jokingly referred to it. The error had been mine, and if anyone was having to bear the consequences, it was me. That's why I immediately wrote off my own wish: a fifth spouse who would be a hybrid of Otis and Runio, a young man who would share clothes and books and the two of them with me. At the same time, though I was ashamed to admit it, I wanted a woman with male genitalia. My desire was so specific that I shrank from making even the slightest suggestion. I said in the end that I wanted an intelligent person. That was all.

Kastra startled me from my daydreaming:

"They're still in bed," she said softly.

"Yep," I replied.

Otis was practically screaming with pleasure.

"He's never been that loud before," Kastra observed.

"He's been holding back. He was angry at Runio."

Kastra cracked her knuckles, then nervously started picking at her scalp again.

"Stop that!" I said, slapping her hand.

For a moment I thought she might cry, but then she grinned.

"Maybe I should go and join them."

"I don't think that's a good idea. Runio is possessive. He doesn't like to share Otis."

"There's no room for jealousy in marriage," Kastra said.

"Of course not, but all's fair in passion."

"The Ministry would disagree. The penalties are severe," she replied.

I looked at her. Kastra started biting her nails.

"Surely you wouldn't report your own husband?" I said slowly.

I was ready to strangle her.

"Of course not."

Her finger was bleeding. She'd chewed her fingernail down to nothing.

"Why did you come to live with us?" I asked.

I couldn't hold my tongue anymore.

"What do you want from us?" I pressed her.

"A family," she said.

"I'm not sure you even know what a family is."

"I know!" she shouted. "I know very well."

She got up and hurried to Otis and Runio. A few moments later, she ran back out of their room crying. She slammed the door to her room. I remained sitting alone. I couldn't understand her.

NIO DIKTER, our fifth spouse, ended up being Kastra's choice. He had a slender physique and wore jewelry. I liked his hands, with their long fingers, and the pronounced veins on his arms. When I saw him, I no longer cared if he was smart.

"No brains, just bits?" Runio asked.

He immediately perceived my hunger. Otis was dissatisfied. He'd wanted a woman.

"Too many men," he said.

Runio agreed. Kastra, however, was beside herself with joy. She didn't want to tell us where she'd found him. Nio Dikter was silent. There was something cruel in his face.

"I'm not so sure he'll save our marriage," Runio said.

Kastra hadn't asked for anyone's opinion. It was already a done deal. "This is Nio Dikter, our husband," she'd said when introducing him to us. Before we could protest, she'd added: "The papers are signed."

That had shut us up, even though I wouldn't have complained too much anyway.

For the first few days, Dikter didn't leave Kastra's room. Otis, Runio, and I didn't know what was going on.

"Maybe she knows him from before?" asked Otis.

"But how? I've never seen him on any list," said Runio. "You know how carefully I read all the columns advertising new spouses."

His dream was to have a large enough family that we could register with the Ministry as a production company. Runio loved Otis, but he loved money even more.

"I know, I know," Otis said. "But maybe you just overlooked him."

"We don't even know his gender," I said. "We don't know what he likes and what he hates. What's he like in bed?"

Runio hugged me.

"Everything will be all right."

"Don't lie to her," Otis said.

We sat in silence. No sound came from Kastra's room.

For days we encountered Kastra and Dikter only in the kitchen. I couldn't determine if they looked happy or not. I waited for a moment when I could be alone with Dikter. I wanted to seduce him, but I could never get a chance. I was on the verge of biting my nails too.

"You want him?" Otis asked me.

Now he was jealous. This was bringing him even closer to Runio. The arrival of Dikter had turned me into a fifth wheel, a free radical. I wasn't happy about it. I wanted everyone's desire to revolve around me, and it revolved, all right, but not in the way I wished. I finally began to understand what had been bothering Kastra over the past months.

In a fit of boredom, I watched all of Runio's footage. His camera seemed to be constantly on, ready to record even the slightest marital tenderness or spite. I watched him flip Otis on his back; I watched as Tarda strangled him in the heat of passion and bit his ears. Then the idea struck me: I could easily mount the camera in Kastra's bedroom. I waited for the opportunity, and as soon as she and Dikter went to the bathroom, I placed the camera on a bookshelf. I even managed to camouflage it.

"What are you up to?" Otis asked me when he saw me emerge.

"I want to participate," I said. "I feel excluded, and you know how curious I am."

Otis grabbed my hand—not Otis, Tarda (I could tell by how tightly he was squeezing)—and pushed me into a room where Runio had already been stripped naked. I'd always been happy between Runio and Tarda, but for some reason my mind kept flitting to the room next door: it pushed me between Dikter and Kastra, who had no space for me. We were two families in one, I thought as my two husbands drifted off to sleep. We were a ménage that Dikter and Kastra had no desire to join. I struggled to fall asleep, as if instead of Runio and Tarda,

I was sharing a bed with two large, cold stone statues. Suddenly what had made me the happiest woman in the world the day before was no longer enough for me.

As was the case with other registered families, our contract with the Ministry required us to pay our taxes using video footage that we sent to the State Archives and uploaded to the Ministry's website. Sex in front of the cameras had become a common means of payment: Otis and Runio bore the brunt of it. They were trying to protect me as much as possible. In the year she'd been with us, Kastra hadn't recorded anything we could cash in on. Her stiff poses and listless facial expressions wouldn't get anyone off.

When we'd registered our family three years before, Otis, Runio, and I had briefly hesitated over which form to fill out: the more common B1, which committed people to filming every moment of their day except for what took place in the bathroom or bedroom, or B2, which only sought explicit material. None of us was an exhibitionist, but not even Runio, the most photogenic, wanted to be in front of the camera all the time.

"When we have children," said Otis, "I don't want perverts watching their every move."

He had a point. So we signed the B2 contract. When he later explained why he'd been attracted to Kastra, Runio said they'd both passionately defended the right to privacy and intimacy. They'd drunk a lot, sure, but she certainly hadn't been lying when she'd said that cameras were evil. Had she said it in front of Otis, we might not have accepted her. Our lives depended on those cameras.

Everyday life was complicated. With the arrival of Nio Dikter, it became even more so. The camera I'd put on their shelf never recorded anything, because the first thing Dikter did was turn it off. It was as if he'd intuitively felt the lens's presence in the room. His insight only made me more excited. He was smart—there was no longer any doubt about it.

After the honeymoon period (to which Kastra was legally entitled), Dikter finally left her room to meet the rest of the family.

"We need to see if there's any chemistry between us," Otis said.

"Of course," Dikter said.

Otis briefly explained what kind of things we were filming.

"We don't make videos every day," he said, "because that would be impossible, but we should record no fewer than three a week. Three is the low end of the scale," he added.

"Understood," Dikter said.

"And now that there are five of us, we ought to make five videos," Otis said.

"Understood," Dikter repeated.

All of his replies were terse. I wondered how it was possible to develop intimacy with someone who spoke so little. Otis, Runio, and I were talkers. I was distrustful of things that remained unsaid. You could get to know a body easily, but the forces that compelled it were difficult to discern in a video. Kastra was beaming the whole time, her hand on Dikter's back. The smile never left her face, this woman whom neither Otis nor Runio nor I could please. I was suspicious. My gaze moved from Dikter's arms to his crotch. He was silent, but Kastra's body language translated him into a language I could easily understand: she looked satisfied. Otis caught me staring and squeezed my shoulder, bringing me back to the conversation.

"Do you have any preferences we should know about?" he asked Dikter. "Is there anything off limits for you?"

"I'm never submissive," he said.

Otis grimaced, but he kept quiet. Runio read the tension in Otis's face and stepped in.

"You and Kastra clicked right away," he said. "Have you recorded anything in the past month?"

"No," said Dikter. "She has to stop biting her nails first. She can't be nervous like that in front of the camera."

The cruelty I'd already detected in him was now apparent.

"You set up the camera in secret, correct?" he asked, looking at me pointedly.

"I did," I said.

"Why?"

"I was curious."

"You can watch," he said, "but not record. Not without my consent."

Tarda was beside himself. All the frustration he'd showered on Runio over the previous year had now found a new victim.

"You're not the boss!" he told him. "She's been here longer than you."

Dikter looked at me. He paid no attention to Otis. He was not swayed by his tone at all.

"Promise me you won't film me without my knowledge."

There was an authority in his voice.

"Okay," I said, "but I want a promise in return."

"What's that?"

"That I can watch whenever I want."

We shook hands. Runio witnessed the deal. Otis and Kastra had left the room. She'd followed him again to comfort him.

WHEN WE'D GOTTEN married, Otis, Runio, and I were never under the delusion that a marital contract meant eternal love. We just wanted to survive. We loved each other, but we were friends above all. Otis and I had met on the Ministry's website. Our profiles matched. Runio contacted us soon after. He shared our enthusiasm for a marriage in which we'd all equally bear the burden of survival and record our sexual activities only when we were really in the mood for it. We were compatible. Our chemistry was strong and our videos were excellent. But the problem was that marriage couldn't restrain people's feelings. It actually stirred them up, and it didn't take long for Runio to develop feelings that Otis couldn't reciprocate. Runio loved me too, but he idolized Otis. His infatuation gained momentum largely due to Otis's dueling personalities, so clearly separate from one another that romantic passion with him was more all-consuming than breathing. Otis Tarda was two lovers in one. Runio couldn't resist him. I could only imagine the moment when, crazed with jealousy over the fact that Otis and I were locked in my room, he'd found perfect revenge in Dorica Kastra. He'd wanted to hurt us, and he'd succeeded.

The days passed, but even though Kastra was buoyed by Dikter's presence, she remained a complete mystery. She seemed to care for Otis, but he seemed not to notice. He couldn't understand why Kastra wouldn't submit to him, why she kept him at a distance. He admitted to me that sometimes he felt she had him on a leash like an obedient dog. She didn't relinquish any control to him. Otis wanted more than anything to see her face in the throes of ecstasy. He wanted her to fall to pieces in his hands, but she wouldn't give in. And when he saw that Kastra had no such reluctance with Dikter, he became even more furious.

"But marriage is like that," I said. "You can't love all people equally. Just accept it."

"I can't," Otis said. "I worship her!"

He sounded like Runio. The tensions in the house only grew. I started doing research on the Ministry's website to see if there were any options for divorce. Some sort of denouement had to happen, though I wasn't entirely sure how we would separate ourselves. Where the head of one began, the genitals of another ended. And my mouth was in the middle of it all.

"Things are getting too complicated," I declared one night in the dining room.

"Yes," Dikter said in his clipped way.

I hadn't even noticed him standing behind me. I didn't know what else to say.

"Are you being satisfied?" he asked me.

"Sure," I said. "I'm not hungry. I have a roof over my head. And two husbands who love me."

"Three husbands," he corrected me.

He didn't even mention Kastra.

"Maybe we were wrong," I said. "Maybe we should've signed contract B1."

"Not at all," Dikter said. "Coming in front of the camera is one thing. Crying in front of it is quite another."

He was right. That certainly would've been unpleasant.

"Has Kastra stopped biting her nails?" I asked.

"Of course," Dikter replied. "Why don't you come see for yourself?"

It was the first opening he'd offered to me since our deal. We'd deliberately avoided each other for weeks to heighten the anticipation. Before I could agree, Otis Tarda entered the room with his nose in the air. Kastra followed him, her head bowed.

"It's time to read the Marquis de Sade! Runio!" he shouted. "Come here!"

It was a family tradition to read erotic works aloud on our anniversary. This time Tarda had chosen *Philosophy in the Bedroom*. After that, we'd exchange gifts, eat dinner, and then all sleep together in the same bed. Tarda's bed was no longer big enough for all of us, however.

"We need to order a bigger mattress," I said.

Runio nodded.

"We're sleeping on the floor tonight," Tarda said. "Naked."

Dikter did not contradict him. Tarda began to read. Dikter and I stared at the floor. Kastra gaped in amazement at Tarda's mouth, from which Sade issued forth like a sermon. She listened to him carefully for the first time. She instantly fell in love with the rigor and playfulness of Tarda's intonation, the resolve with which he spat the Marquis's words on Christianity and marital relations. There was something funny about all of it, and I laughed. Tarda looked at me reproachfully.

"Take off your clothes," he ordered.

But Kastra began to strip instead of me.

"What are you doing?" Tarda asked her.

"You still haven't seen me completely naked. I want you to fully know me."

When her clothes fell to the floor, Tarda was left speechless. Sade fell out of his hands. Kastra let out a loud sigh and fell to her knees. She held the book gently to her chest, and then presented it to Tarda. As soon as her hands were free, she slid them into his pants and began to moan. We'd never seen her like that.

"Tarda," said Dikter. "Keep reading."

Otis obliged him. When he arrived at the sentence "Do you see this libertine discharge mentally, without anyone having touched her?" I cackled, and Kastra burst out sobbing. She'd finally lost control. Pleasure twisted her face. She came with a shriek. It was only then that I noticed Dikter was holding a camera in his lap. "She's earned her first paycheck," he said.

Kastra was sitting on the floor. Beneath her was a small puddle. Otis was proud. He stroked her face. Runio stroked him. The spirit of the Marquis de Sade entered our family as the sixth member. I immediately fell to dreaming of a seventh person. I wrapped a lock of hair around my index finger and gazed off into the distance. Kastra had come from hearing literature read out loud. But I needed people. Lots of them.

The Sorrows of Young Lotte

Oh, you who bore her to me and my love,
Hold you her, mother, embraced;
thrice be you blessed for me!
Thrice blessed be your heart, feeling the same,
Which first gave to your child
the tenderness of womankind!
>   —FRIEDRICH GOTTLIEB KLOPSTOCK,
>   "THE FUTURE BELOVED"

June

The moment you set eyes on me is decisive for us both: I'm slicing black bread and sharing the pieces with my brothers and sisters. You conclude I'm a generous person. Big mistake. Everything my mother denied me, I'm inclined to take from others—but that's not obvious upon first glance. I'm beautifully dressed, ready to dance. I look lovely. You like my white dress adorned with red ribbons. You're not indifferent to my gloves with their tiny pearl clasps at the wrist. We simultaneously look up at the sky, knowing that inclement weather will soon spoil the party. I'm looking forward to the downpour. I've worn white because it looks best when drenched. You can't even begin to fathom my wickedness. The bread I eat is always black.

We talk about literature. I falsely claim that my favorite authors are those who write realistically about my existence.

"Country life isn't perfect," I say, "but for me, it is a wellspring of happiness."

I lie to your face, but you're convinced that Beauty and Truth are one and the same, and I'm quite stunning. I praise Klopstock. You concur. You look into my eyes while thinking of my ass. We debate nonsense. We haven't yet arrived at the ball, but we've been dancing a verbal minuet. We dance, but we don't touch. It's still too soon for that. When you finally manage to touch me, I'll make sure you regret it. I smile, but my good spirits say nothing about me.

Once in the ballroom we dance a waltz, cruelty spinning us in a circle. I feel the possessive grip of your hands. You're so excited you're not breathing. Your desire is like a velvet skirt, bigger and heavier than it looks. And I, too, am heavy, but you're convinced you can carry me across the floor with ease. Clearly you don't know women.

We go for a walk afterward. When we sit down, you give me two oranges. You're preoccupied with these oranges—you don't want me to share them. For each segment I eat, I give one to the person beside me. What a sweet grimace you make! I thrust the knife straight into your heart and wait. I don't want to push it all the way in yet. You deserve to be tortured.

When, after the intermission, we dance again,

I make sure to draw near to my old neighbor who adores Albert and takes every opportunity to mention him. I want you to hear his name: once, twice. It doesn't escape your attention. Right away you ask who he is. I time my answer; we part in a figure eight and the words remain at the tip of my tongue. I prolong your agony. I furrow my brow. I act like I don't want to hurt you.

"Albert is my fiancé," I say.

You trip over your own feet, confused. You dance terribly. Only the handle can be seen now at your chest.

I want you to at least get a glimpse of my rich inner life. When it finally starts to storm and other guests come inside to escape the rain, I propose a parlor game that will clearly reveal my character.

"Listen!" I say. "I'll go around you in a circle, clockwise, and you'll count off, quickly. Whoever stutters or miscounts gets slapped."

I move fast, then faster, slapping my neighbors and acquaintances. I hit you twice as hard as anyone else. Your cheeks redden. I want to say, "Werther, what a fool you are!" because it's obvious you're enjoying it.

After the game, I stand by the window. Outside, the rain splashes against the ground. The wind gusts and makes my eyes tear. You think I'm crying from intense emotion. You bend over and kiss the hand that slapped you. You look into my eyes. You've understood nothing.

Ten days later, you call my mother's children

mine. You say: Charlotte's children. You roll around on the floor with my brothers. You look like a pig. You are a pig. I race into the kitchen and stuff a piece of ham in my mouth. I imagine devouring your salted thigh.

July

Let us begin the month with your deepest fears: first, the possibility of losing me; and second, getting a job. You enjoy, as you've told me in confidence, planting spinach and other vegetables. You'd rather be doing that. You refuse your mother's exhortations to take up a diplomatic post. Your only duty is to visit me all the time, sit with me for hours, and accompany me on nature walks. You advocate for a simple, provincial life. Wherever you go, you defend pastoral pleasure and innocence, but inside you're a ball of yarn that unwinds at the sight of the worst depravity and suffering. After all, you're an upstanding German citizen.

You stubbornly lie to yourself about the lust you feel in my presence. You deceive yourself into believing you love me more profoundly than those women who were good for some passing fun in the provinces. But we both know what you're thinking about when you hold heads of cabbage in your hands. You praise my musical and literary tastes, but you try drawing me naked when you go home. Our discussions of Lessing are superfluous. A drawing of my silhouette is enough.

At night you kiss the notes I send you. Your servant told me as much. You don't know that I stick them under my naked buttocks while I play the piano. You think that the courier folded them, but no—they crumpled under my weight. You long to be every chair I sit on, but you can't admit it. You are, after all, a delicate specimen. You express yourself in the vocative like a poet.

When Albert finally returns from his trip at the end of July, your impotence has reached its peak. As soon as we're left alone, you praise him: my, how sensitive Albert is, ah, how much he loves me, oh, how intelligent and dignified! Everything you want to say about yourself, you project onto him. When you see him, you instantly become hysterical, laughing loudly and cracking jokes. You're a sick man. You think I'll take care of you until you get better, but women aren't cold compresses, we're icy whirlwinds that ignite fevers. It's not in my interest for you to recover, ever. There's only one outcome: death.

August

You want to be a member of my family, but you don't know my relatives at all. You don't know my father and his feigned kindness. You didn't know my mother, who was an inexhaustible source of other people's suffering and discomfort. You've imposed yourself on us; you want to be father to my brothers and sisters. You want them to be our children, for us to raise them together. These are not my wants. I don't want to play house. That's not the minuet I like. When I can't catch my breath in the circle of my family, it's never due to joyful spinning.

While we're picking pears together in the garden, my thoughts turn to your conversation with Albert, which he recounted to me later. You took down his pistol from the wall and wanted to shoot yourself in the head. He argued that suicide was stupid. You passionately defended your position, that there's a limit to how much sorrow a man can endure. You told him that love was also a sickness, one that it was all right to die from.

You said, "It's all right to give up." Even though, truth be told, you wouldn't give up even in death.

I regret, of course, that Albert's pistol wasn't loaded. Only gunpowder would blast those stupid prejudices from your head.

PS
At the end of the month we celebrate your birthday. Albert buys you a book you want. Before he sends it, I sneak into the package the red ribbon I was wearing the night we met. You're already standing on the edge of the abyss. You just need a gentle push.

September
I can talk about my mother only at nighttime because the memory of her is an evil that can't bear even the slightest trace of light. She bore so

many children and gave so little love to the world! She manipulated all of us. Albert knows this well. He's never judged my hatred. Motherhood is holy to you, however, and whenever I mention my mother, you think I'm speaking of her with admiration. You love your mother. You ignore her, but you love her. I imagine the tenderness with which she raised her favorite. I could never take her place, nurturing your weakness like it's the greatest gift to humanity. You're not suited for life. You're constantly daydreaming. You draw me naked, you long for Albert to die. You convince yourself I care. I don't want to free you from your delusion; you deserve unrequited love. You deserve a mother like mine.

On her deathbed my mother asked me to be a servile wife to my own father! To be a mother to my own brothers! Sometimes when I pass by her bedroom, I go in and secretly spit on her bed. You remind me of her. Behind your sensitivity lurks a devious mind. Albert is a saint compared to you. His roughness stays in the bedroom where I can easily bear it.

At the beginning of the month we stand beneath a chestnut tree, moonlight illuminating the path that you walk with me by day. I babble on about some foolishness. I'm upset. You grasp at every word I utter about death.

"We will meet again," you say, certain I want to hear it.

While he accompanies me home, Albert and I discuss how much I despise you. Later he slips through the open window into my room. He chokes me to help me relax.

October, November, December, January, February, March, April, May, June

Is a woman even alive if there's no man nearby lamenting his pain in her presence? Of course, but who cares? You flee to go work for a nobleman. Albert and I get married.

One of the wedding guests says, "What a shame that Walter isn't here."

People have forgotten your name. They've buried you alive.

July

We didn't get to throw a handful of dirt on you; you've already come back from the dead. You've returned with your tail between your legs. You notice how Albert clasps me around the waist. You're consumed with jealousy. I was right: you're an evil man.

August

I write a few letters to my relatives. I want to escape. Albert says it's not a bad idea, but my father, my brothers, they look at me dejectedly. They howl like village dogs tethered to a tree. Who would slice their bread if I left? Whose hand would they eat from if not mine?

You come by constantly. Albert laughs. Your intrusiveness flatters him. Sometimes your tears are a salve for the bruises Albert leaves on my body, especially the thighs you furtively touched. For every one of your inappropriate touches and glances, Albert later punishes me. I've come close to thanking you openly. Your desire has strengthened our marriage.

September

Let's finally get to the glorification of those people you refer to in conversation as "the raw and uneducated class." You praise the peasants by insulting them. You say you're a worse person than they are because you're "educated," but if you think about it—were not the peasants and the philistines educated by the same mother who always says yes to her sons, while repeating no to her daughters?

You applaud the servant who tried to rape his mistress because to you such an outburst of passion is healthy and genuine, while scruples are a sign of bourgeois affliction. But then with unconcealed contempt you tell Albert the peasant women are too promiscuous. You celebrate me, the educated and happy, and spit on them, the uneducated and happy. And why, for the love of God, don't you say openly that you want to rape me but that your reading of Klopstock holds you back? I don't think it's right to blame one's own impulses on poets, however pathetic they are. There's nothing romantic about ignorance and rural coarseness. I've told you this countless times. But I can't dissuade you. You ardently defend your position that education has made us rigid, that it prevents us from reacting in the ways we really want. Albert and I read between the lines: you are ready for a cruelty from which no woman could ever recover.

When Albert controls my breathing, he observes the color of my face. He follows my inhalations and exhalations. You would stare into my eyes, watching yourself in them. You would strangle me, just so you could have me forever. It's all the same to you whether I'm alive or dead. The question of life for you is a trifle that preoccupies only good-natured and dull-witted provincials. You are above mere survival. Death is more precious to the philistine. Especially the death of a woman. You think you're so refined, but the cabbage doesn't lie. The head of cabbage is the same whether it's picked by the rough, cracked hands of the peasant or the well-groomed hands of the salon philosopher. I am that cabbage. I feed all of you, but only Albert cares about my appetites.

You intercept my message to Albert (I wrote that I could hardly wait for him to come home). You muse aloud that I wrote it to you. Usually I have no trouble hiding my feelings, but this time my face betrays my disgust. You clearly see how much your comment has annoyed me. I hate when I briefly lose control, when I can't master my emotions. Especially in the presence of vile men who pretend they're in my power. Right away I go write to Albert that I can't endure another minute in your company and he suggests I go to him by coach. It takes me two days to recover my peace of mind. While I'm away from home, I realize I need to do something. I can't stand you anymore. I'll just wait for you to attack me, so that Albert challenges you to a duel. If you can't pull the trigger yourself, the gunpowder should be given to someone else to finish the job. To provoke you even further, I buy a canary and feed it bread in front of you. I give it crumbs from my mouth. My message is clear. You turn your head. You know, deep down, that I'd even give an animal what I'd never give you: crumbs of tenderness, the tiniest kindness.

Your nerves are fraying. You're full of rage. They cut down two trees, walnut trees you loved. You attacked the priest's wife for this. You wanted to choke her. You scream about it in front of me, in front of Albert, even in front of my father. Everyone here knows that neither the priest nor his wife should venture out. Although both trees stood on their property, you say, "MY WALNUT TREES." I'm no longer a head of cabbage. I've become a felled tree.

October

You admire authority figures, princes, literary giants, and Albert. I don't know how Albert ended up in this group, given that he has no interest in being a father figure; he doesn't want complicated relationships with children.

November

While we're celebrating Albert's birthday, I notice how much you're drinking. You're disappearing into your glass. You've kept your mouth shut, but your eyes are giving you away. You look at Albert as if your pupils are a pair of daggers. You brush up against my dress more often; you let your hands roam freely. I'm not sure how much of it is conscious and how much is driven by wine.

I enjoy drinking, too, but not in front of you. My tongue would surely untie. That was how I confessed to Albert years ago that I wanted him and explained, in detail, what I expected of him. I was young when we met, but I already knew what I wanted. Wine doesn't have the same effect on you. Even if you drank the entire cask, you wouldn't confess what you're after. Albert knows. That's why we're here: happy in your misery.

I tell you that you should stop drinking so much, but not out of concern. The things you do, other men did before you. The same looks, the same touches. The same breath and the same lies they called Truth. I am, unfortunately, well acquainted with this "love." You don't know the difference between tenderness and violence. The wine's not to blame, but rather mothers, who, together with poets, bear some responsibility. After the other guests disperse, you stay seated at the table with me and Albert. You talk about poets. You don't mention your mother.

"When I read poets of yore and recognize in them my own heart, how torturous it is! I never knew that people before us were so miserable, that they suffered as much as we do."

You don't slur your words. You sound sober.

"Everyone suffers, Werther," says Albert. "You're not the only one."

"But you suffer less than others. You have Lotte."

"She's not a talisman," he says, his voice clipped.

"You should carry her in your heart," you say. "Like I do. Then she will be."

Albert laughs. He's not angry. He points to his head and says, "I carry her here."

"Me too!" you say, and smack your forehead loudly.

I'm sick of your conversation. When I get up from the table, you begin to vomit. Finally I get a closer look at what's inside you. It's revolting.

In the days that follow, you show more openly how much you want me. You're no longer suppressing it. You stare at me, quoting significant verses. You make a point of coming by when Albert's not home. I sit at the piano, playing and singing to exhaustion, just to avoid talking to you. Here and there you cry out loud; you're done holding back. Your feelings are plain to see. If only you'd keep on about your vegetable garden, you wouldn't feel the need to cry so much!

December

My musicality goes far beyond the minuet, the waltz, or any other virtuosic piano piece. The sound I enjoy most is the slap of an open palm on a bare ass. The same sound I made with my hand when I slapped you at last year's dance. I'm sure you haven't forgotten it. I'm thinking about repeating those slaps. Albert tells me you encountered Henrik on a walk. You recognized him instantly. You sympathize with him; you think he went insane because of me.

"Lotte's eyes drove him crazy," you say.

"You're talking nonsense," Albert replies. "She has nothing to do with him."

My father employed Henrik as a clerk when my mother was still alive. It wasn't long before he wrote his first love letter to me. The paper always displayed the traces of his tears. Clerks are odd creatures. They're not writers, but they, too, lack imagination. I was sick of his pathetic sentences and red-faced looks full of longing.

Once, when my father wasn't home, I went looking for my mother to complain about my brothers banging on my piano. The door to her room was ajar and I saw—though it was the last thing I wanted to see—Henrik the clerk lying on top of her. My mother was stretched out on her stomach and didn't notice me. They were both panting loudly. At first I heard only the piano, the strains of children's songs being pounded out on the keys. I was distraught. Mama was getting louder and louder, but I couldn't hear her voice, just the slapping sound of her buttocks, which could never be inscribed in sheet music.

Henrik continued to court me after that. While I'd play piano, he'd sit nearby. He came over every day for lunch. He touched me under the table.

"He's very industrious," said my father.

My mother agreed. "Tireless," she said.

Henrik was domesticated in no time. The affection he and my mother exchanged in bed nearly began to show in public, in front of her numerous children, even in front of her husband. It was completely repulsive, the way he addressed me in my mother's presence. Maybe he wanted to make her jealous? I begged my father to let me visit my cousins, and he gladly consented to it. Nothing escaped my father. He knew everything. He saw everything. When I returned from my trip, he brusquely reported that Henrik was not well and needed to leave his post. He'd fired him.

"After you left," my father said, "the young man went completely crazy."

His words spread throughout the neighborhood. Everyone began to look at me reproachfully.

"My son was sound and healthy before he went to work for you," repeated his mother. "Charlotte drove him to the madhouse."

When you came upon him, his mother was there too. What exactly did she say? That he was an exemplary, even-tempered son, who out of nowhere had grown melancholy, come down with a fever, and ended up in an asylum? You seized on her words because you think I'm mortal danger. Peasant women are a venereal disease. I'm a disease of the soul.

To the Reader, from Albert

Charlotte doesn't want to hear Werther's name anymore, and she asked me to take her place in relating to you what happened. She told me, "Albert, you're a lawyer and you don't know how to write, but it's better if you bore the reader than if I do."

When I first met Lotte, I knew right away that she was a genius. She was only sixteen years old, but she already knew far more than I did. When she would speak fervently of Lessing, for example, her eyebrows would go up and down. She was both dramatic and composed, and I fell in love with her at once. I didn't hide it from her; we'd known one another barely a month when I admitted that I loved her and thought of her more often than my own mother, and I thought of my mother quite often. My inappropriate joke pleased her, because her mother was an awful woman. We became best friends. Whenever I'd travel for work, I'd write her long letters and send books she'd requested. Lotte would read the books and then we'd engage in an epistolary debate about them, or about the latest gossip. We didn't always agree. For example, I loved Klopstock, but she found him repugnant. She always interpreted popular works through the lens of local political conditions. Poetry was never just a text to sigh over for her. I wish I could explain to you in her words the problem she had with poets, but that's not possible. It's hard to find better words than hers. She was precise in her language and in her desires.

She asked me to marry her first, while we were foraging for wild mushrooms in the forest. I accepted immediately. Then she said that once we'd gathered enough thick and juicy mushrooms, I should take some to her father and ask him to compensate me with his thick and juicy daughter. I froze. Her father didn't have much of a sense of humor, but Lotte said everything would be fine: he knew, she said, that she would still look after the children. She was right. Her father accepted but asked us to postpone the wedding because Lotte was "too young" for marriage. She was twenty years old. Anyway, I don't mean to bore you with the details, but the situation with Werther was getting worse and worse. Lotte said she somehow needed to fix it. He was bothering her too much. I agreed that

Werther had become a pest, but I didn't offer to talk to him. I knew Lotte would find her own solution. She didn't need to say, *Albert, let me deal with this on my own*. I told her not to procrastinate too much because Werther was only getting more brazen.

I was sometimes jealous of the way Werther would say "we" when speaking about Charlotte and himself. For instance, he bragged about mushroom foraging "again" with Lotte: "We have to go pick mushrooms again" is how he said it. When I complained about his behavior, Lotte told me not to be jealous because she planned to gather a special kind of mushroom for him. I told her she mustn't poison him, and she replied, "Maybe I'll have to." In the meantime, a peasant whom Werther would meet now and then at the tavern killed the servant of a widow he was in love with and had previously tried to rape. Werther rushed to help him, identifying with his violence. He begged the manager to set the killer free. "He did it in a fit of passion!" shouted Werther. The man had been in love with the widow for years. He'd killed her servant out of jealousy. "You must take pity on him!" Lotte was visibly unnerved when I recounted the story to her. "He didn't kill the widow," I said, "just her servant," but Charlotte said it didn't matter. He'd killed a person. He'd given Werther an idea.

I knew that Lotte was right because at one point, Werther took up his friend's defense in the plural: "*We* men are passionate creatures!" I trembled at his words. I didn't recognize myself in them. When she was upset, Charlotte would go into the kitchen, prepare a heap of food, and eat until she calmed down. Her mother had often berated her for this. Her father had rebuked her, too, but it didn't bother me. I wasn't going to tell her how to feel. I'd sit in silence at the table and eat with her. And this time I did the same. She told me between mouthfuls that if she didn't kill Werther, he would kill me. I replied that I knew this because he defended the killer with such passion that I occasionally felt sorry for him. Lotte said I should under no circumstances pity him. She chewed slowly. She said, "If only he'd shoot at my father like Henrik did!" Lotte condemned all brutes, not just Werther. She'd once written that she lived in an environment that valued conspicuous male violence and inconspicuous female cruelty. Men fired pistols. Women gathered poisonous mushrooms. Lotte didn't want to accept such a role. She understood both motherhood and gunpowder. Her life, she wrote to me, did not begin and end with hoeing vegetables and birthing children. In any case, Lotte wandered off somewhere in her thoughts while we were eating. I asked her what she was going to do. She stared at a piece of ham. I jokingly asked if she planned to kill and eat Werther. Lotte made a disgusted grunt and pushed away the meat. She got up from her chair and left.

When Lotte returned home that night, she was covered in blood. I helped her remove her clothes, then warmed some water to bathe her. I dried her hair and threw her dirty clothes in the fire. Knowing that she'd been planning something, I'd sent all the servants into the city a couple hours earlier with a long list of tasks that would keep them occupied for at least two days. There was no one in the kitchen. Still, I didn't ask her what she'd done. I just hugged her and told her everything would be all right. "Of course it will," Lotte said. She shivered and I helped her get dressed. She had no trouble falling asleep. I went out to groom my horse and wash the traces of blood from his back and neck. Just before dawn I found Lotte at her writing desk. She pushed a letter into my hand and said she'd explained everything in detail. I nodded. When she left the room, I sat in her spot next to the fireplace and began to read. Outside a heavy snow was falling. I wondered whether she'd left any tracks.

Dear Albert,

I didn't tell you this sooner in order to avoid upsetting you, but a few days ago, while I was sitting at the piano, Werther pounced on me after crying over some stupid song. I pushed him off and barely managed to escape to the next room. I locked the door, which he was bearing down on. Werther repeated that he loved me, and that he wouldn't leave until he could see me and hear my voice.

"You want to rape me!"

He insisted this wasn't true.

"I just want to see you. Talk to me!"

I wiped away his kisses with my hand. I felt nauseous and vomited on the parquet floor.

"All right," I said after catching my breath. "But I can't see you now because I'm overcome with passion. Albert would catch us in an embrace."

"Tell me, my love, tell me when can we meet? When can I kiss you again?"

"Soon," I said. "Don't come here anymore, lest Albert suspect something. I'll have one of my servants bring you a note and we can meet in the forest."

"Oh, my love," moaned Werther. "I am your only servant!"

Another wave of nausea stopped me from speaking further. Thankfully a servant came into the room and I heard the lout leave in a hurry.

"You can come out," said a woman's voice. "He's gone."

She cleaned the floor and I was sure she knew what had happened. All the women in the village were familiar with Werther and his high-minded city impulses. We didn't utter a word; we understood each other in silence.

Then the murder happened. I needed to urgently reconceive my plan. After you and I had lunch in the kitchen I went to write Werther a message: "Dearest, I know you're sad for your friend. Let my gentle kisses soothe your endless suffering tonight, and calm your trembling heart!"

Werther replied immediately: "My beloved, my one and only, the sorrow of my heart, come comfort me! Your servant needs you and kisses you endlessly!"

Never, since we'd first met, had I extended the slightest tenderness to him, but all the same he clung to my promise as if I'd been passionately loving him my whole life. I grabbed a weapon, but not the one from the wall, rather the pistol you'd hidden in the book on the Code of Hammurabi. First I went for a walk to clear my head. My plan was simple: I needed to knock out Werther with a small dose of poison and discharge the pistol into his empty head. I was nervous. Much time had passed since my mother's death, but the memory of her was still alive. And Werther's face would persecute me just as hers did. I nearly lost my courage when I ran into Henrik's mother. I wanted to bypass her, but she gripped my hand and insulted me. Fortunately her son was nowhere in sight. It was cold; she'd surely put him in a warm bed and left him to his beautiful dreams. Her slander returned me to the time when, instead of Werther, her son had tormented me. I tore my hand away from her and fled.

"Witch!" she shouted after me.

You know how much I hate that word. I hate it with a passion equal to Werther's hatred of women.

When I returned home, I didn't let you know, but

rather went directly to the horse and made off for Werther's place. He was waiting for me in a robe. In his hand was the red ribbon I'd gifted him for his birthday. He wrapped it around his finger.

"That ribbon belonged to my late mother," I said.

He didn't hear me. The smile never left his face. He was so self-confident it made me sick, but I needed to be patient.

"Have you any wine?" I asked.

"Of course," said Werther.

He brought two glasses. I noticed one of them was chipped. I poured the poison into that one while his back was turned.

"Where has your man gone?" I asked.

The house was quiet.

"He's around here somewhere," he lied.

I considered how months of Werther's greedy hands and sweet talk had prepared me for this moment. I knew that if I changed my mind, he would never give up.

"How will Albert react when he finds out about us?"

He didn't expect an answer. He was talking to himself. In fact, he was talking to you. I was sure he wanted you to watch us.

I slowly took the ribbon from Werther's hand and tied it around the wine glass.

"Imagine this glass is me."

I offered it to him. I expected him to empty it, but Werther was a scoundrel like me. He hesitated.

"Let the first sip be yours, and then I'll drink from the place touched by your lips."

I had no choice, so I drank a little wine. I handed the glass back to him.

"And now you!" I said.

My tone was too sharp so I quickly added, "Dearest Werther, my love, take the wine as you will take me."

I spoke such drivel, the German poets would have envied me.

"There's time," said Werther.

I won't lie, I was scared. I expected him to attack me at any minute, but he seemed not to be in a hurry.

"Do you remember the day we met?"

"Of course I remember!" I said. "I'll never forget. We spoke at length about literature."

"Yes," said Werther. "You praised Klopstock enthusiastically."

"Well, he's marvelous!"

"Interesting. Your father told me recently that you don't like him—indeed, he said you despise him."

He sounded cold and suspicious.

"My father doesn't know me at all."

I blinked a few times, very seductively, but it was as if Werther were looking right through me.

"I spoke with Henrik too. He's crazy, but very smart."

"Ah, poor, sweet Henrik! Life has been so unfair to him."

"Life, or you?"

The poison was beginning to take effect.

"Can I sit down? The mention of him always saddens me."

"Go ahead," said Werther.

"I wouldn't say he went crazy because of me. He loved older women."

"Your mother?" he asked.

"I didn't know you'd become so close with my father," I said.

"I can drink a lot. Your father, not so much."

I wanted to change the subject.

"My mother was a wonderful person. Everyone loved her."

"Your father said you resemble her."

"If only!" I lied. "She was a true beauty."

Werther removed his robe and stood before me. He was completely naked.

"If she wasn't modest, then I guess you aren't either," he said.

"My mother was very pious and wouldn't have tolerated such behavior," I lied.

I laughed, though I wanted to cry.

"My beautiful Lotte," said Werther, taking my face in his hand.

He dropped it to my neck, moving lower and lower. I grew frightened that he'd see the scars. The bruises on my shoulders were quite visible, but fortunately, he stopped at my décolletage. Werther was, like Henrik, the most ordinary boor.

"More wine?" he asked.

"You know I never drink," I said.

"You drink, just not in front of me."

"What exactly did my father tell you?"

"He admitted he doesn't like Albert."

"That I know," I said.

"I don't like him either."

The quiet was becoming unbearable. I went to get up, but Werther held me down roughly in the armchair.

"Stay seated," he said.

He removed the ribbon from the glass and tied it around my neck. I felt for my pistol. Before I could take it out and blow away his genitals, which were hanging right in front of my nose, Werther sank into the armchair across from mine and finally brought the chipped glass of wine to his lips. He gulped it down.

"Do you love Albert?" he asked.

There was no reason to lie anymore.

"More than anything."

He gazed into the distance. The wine was slowly putting him to sleep.

"While I was at my diplomatic post, I found your doppelgänger and did everything to her that I wanted to do to you, but it didn't help."

"Is that why you returned, to finish the job?"

Werther didn't answer. His head slumped on the back of the chair.

I tried calling to him loudly, "Werther! Werther!"

He didn't respond. I shook him. It was over. I dressed him slowly in his favorite clothes. I forged his handwriting and wrote Werther's farewell letter to me. When I pressed the pistol against his temple, he opened his eyes for a moment. There wasn't a shred of horror on his face. Midnight struck and I fired. I didn't wait to see if he was dead. If he didn't die right away, I reckoned he'd surely be gone by morning. I planted the pistol in his right hand. I hurried out into the night air, mounted the horse, and took off. The crime had been prevented. You already know the condition I was in when I came home. When the messenger comes today to inform us of his death, I plan to faint. I've firmly decided. I didn't cry enough when my mother died. That was a mistake. For Werther I will sob twice as hard, thrice. Her life hangs by a thread, people will say, and you know all too well how quickly gossip travels. Everyone will think that I truly died with him.

Translator Acknowledgments

The translator would like to credit the below sources and translators for their work reproduced in this book:

—Quotes on pages 45 and 183: Marquis de Sade, *Justine, Philosophy in the Bedroom, & Other Writings*, trans. Richard Seaver and Austryn Wainhouse (New York: Grove Press, 1965).

—Poem on page 156: Georg Trakl, "Elis," trans. Mirza Purić (unpublished, 2022).

—Poem on pages 159 and 160: George Trakl, "To the Boy Elis," trans. Bob Herz, *Nine Mile Magazine*'s *Talk About Poetry* (blog), *Nine Mile Magazine*, March 29, 2016, https://talkaboutpoetry. wordpress.com/2016/03/29/trakl-the-elis-poems/.

—Poem on page 162: George Trakl, "Elis," trans. Bob Herz, *Nine Mile Magazine*'s *Talk About Poetry* (blog), *Nine Mile Magazine*, March 29, 2016, https://talkaboutpoetry.wordpress. com/2016/03/29/trakl-the-elis-poems/.

—Epigraph on page 185: Friedrich Gottlieb Klopstock, "The Future Beloved," trans. Anne Posten (unpublished, 2022).

ASJA BAKIĆ is a Bosnian/Croatian author of poetry and prose, as well as a translator. She was selected as one of Literary Europe Live's New Voices from Europe 2017, and her writing has been translated into seven languages. Her debut, *Mars*, was published in English by the Feminist Press in 2019. She currently lives and works in Zagreb, Croatia.

JENNIFER ZOBLE translates Balkan literature into English. Recent books include *Call Me Esteban*, her translation of *Zovite me Esteban* by Lejla Kalamujić, and her translation of *Mars* by Asja Bakić, which was named one of the "Best Fiction Books of 2019" by *Publishers Weekly*. Zoble is on the faculty of Liberal Studies at NYU, where she teaches writing and translation.

More Translated Literature from the Feminist Press

The Age of Goodbyes by Li Zi Shu,
translated by YZ Chin

Arid Dreams: Stories by Duanwad Pimwana,
translated by Mui Poopoksakul

La Bastarda by Trifonia Melibea Obono,
translated by Lawrence Schimel

**Blood Feast: The Complete Short Stories
of Malika Moustadraf**
translated by Alice Guthrie

Cockfight by María Fernanda Ampuero,
translated by Frances Riddle

Grieving: Dispatches from a Wounded Country
by Cristina Rivera Garza,
translated by Sarah Booker

In Case of Emergency by Mahsa Mohebali,
translated by Mariam Rahmani

Mars: Stories by Asja Bakić,
translated by Jennifer Zoble

Panics by Barbara Molinard,
translated by Emma Ramadan

Violets by Kyung-Sook Shin,
translated by Anton Hur

The Feminist Press publishes books that ignite movements and social transformation. Celebrating our legacy, we lift up insurgent and marginalized voices from around the world to build a more just future.

See our complete list of books at
feministpress.org

THE FEMINIST PRESS
AT THE CITY UNIVERSITY OF NEW YORK
FEMINISTPRESS.ORG